SEAL MY LOVE

A SEAL Brotherhood Novel

SHARON HAMILTON

SHARON HAMILTON'S BOOK LIST

SEAL BROTHERHOOD SERIES

SEAL Encounter (Prequel Novella)
Accidental SEAL (Book 1)
SEAL Endeavor (Novella)
Fallen SEAL Legacy (Book 2)
SEAL Under Covers (Book 3)
SEAL The Deal (Book 4)
Cruisin' For A SEAL (Book 5)
SEAL My Destiny (Book 6)
SEAL Of My Heart (Book 7)
SEAL My Love (Book 9)
SEAL Brotherhood Box Set 1 (Accidental SEAL & Prequel)
SEAL Brotherhood Box Set 2 (Fallen SEAL & Prequel)
Ultimate SEAL Collection Vol. 1 (Books 1-4 + 2 Prequels)
Ultimate SEAL Collection Vol. 2 (Books 5-7)

BAD BOYS OF SEAL TEAM 3 SERIES

SEAL's Promise (Book 1)
SEAL My Home (Book 2)
SEAL's Code (Book 3)
Big Bad Boys Bundle (Books 1-3 of Bad Boys)

BAND OF BACHELORS SERIES

Lucas (Book 1)
Alex (Book 2)
Jake (Book 3)
Jake 2 (Book 4)
Band of Bachelors Bundle (Books 1-4)

TRUE BLUE SEALS SERIES

True Navy Blue (prequel to Zak)
Zak (Includes novella above)

NASHVILLE SEAL SERIES

Nashville SEAL (Book 1)

Nashville SEAL: Jameson (Books 1 & 2 combined)

FREDO SERIES

Fredo's Secret (novella) Book 1

Fredo's Dream (Books 1 & 2 combined)

STANDALONE NOVELLAS

SEAL You In My Dreams (Magnolias and Moonshine)

SEAL Of Time (Trident Legacy)

KINDLE WORLDS

SEAL's Goal: The Beautiful Game

Love Me Tender, Love You Hard

PARADISE SERIES

Paradise: In Search of Love

SLEEPER SEALS

Bachelor SEAL

BONE FROG BROTHERHOOD SERIES

New Years SEAL Dream

FALL FROM GRACE SERIES (PARANORMAL)

Gideon: Heavenly Fall

GOLDEN VAMPIRES OF TUSCANY SERIES (PARANORMAL)

Honeymoon Bite (Book 1)

Mortal Bite (Book 2)

THE GUARDIANS (PARANORMAL)

Heavenly Lover (Book 1)

Underworld Lover (Book 2)

Underworld Queen (Book 3)

AUTHOR'S NOTE

I always dedicate my SEAL Brotherhood books to the brave men and women who defend our shores and keep us safe. Without their sacrifice—and that of their families, because a warrior's fight always includes his or her family—I wouldn't have the freedom and opportunity to make a living writing these stories. They sometimes pay the ultimate price so we can debate, argue, go have coffee with friends, raise our children, and see them have children of their own.

One of my favorite tributes to warriors resides on many memorials, including one I saw honoring the fallen of WWII on an island in the Pacific:

"When you go home
Tell them of us, and say
For your tomorrow,
We gave our today."

These are my stories created out of my own imagination. Anything that is inaccurately portrayed is either my mistake or done intentionally to disguise something I might have heard over a beer or in the corner of one of the hangouts along the Coronado Strand.

In the interest of full disclosure, portions of this book were briefly featured in a multi-author anthology no longer available, titled *Tropical Tryst*. The portions that appeared previously have been substantially updated, added to, and re-edited to reflect new story choices and changes.

I support two main charities. Navy SEAL/UDT Museum operates in Ft. Pierce, Florida. Please learn about this wonderful museum, all run by active and former SEALs and their friends and families, and who rely on public support, not that of the U.S. Government. www.navysealmuseum.org

I also support Wounded Warriors, who tirelessly bring together the warrior as well as the family members who are just learning to deal with their soldier's condition and have nowhere to turn. It is a long path to becoming well, but I've seen first-hand what this organization does for its warriors and the families who love them. Please give what your heart tells you is right. If you cannot give, volunteer at one of the many service centers all over the United States. Get involved. Do something meaningful for someone who gave so much of themselves, to families who have paid the price for your freedom. You'll find a family there unlike any other on the planet. www.woundedwarriorproject.org

CHAPTER 1

NAVY SEAL TRACE Bennett sat down on one of the benches at Gunny's Gym, picked up a thirty pound barbell, and started his reps, focusing on a straight back and neck so he didn't pay for it later tonight. He'd been told it was mandatory to do daily PT when they were between deployments. Unless he wanted to do a cool ten-mile run or a swim in the inlet, it was Gunny's, and a great place to get to know some of the other guys. Since the Team had just come back from a short mission to Baja California, they weren't likely to be sent out again for several months, unless something flared up. And that happened a lot lately.

Being the newest member of Kyle Lansdowne's squad on SEAL Team 3, his transfer from Team 8 had been hastened by a messy divorce and a bad write-up on his interim evaluation. He'd told his LPO that he just needed a change of scenery.

"Lansdowne runs a tight ship. They watch for

cracks. You wanna stay in as a SEAL, you better not have one," said Sr. Chief Masterson.

That had brought a smile to his lips.

Masterson barked back at him. "Fuckin' pervert! I didn't mean your butt crack, Bennett. I mean your head's gotta be *right*, but I'm with most my peers in this. If you can't fuck, you can't fight. So I guess I should feel grateful you at least have a sense of humor and a dirty mind. That's a good sign."

"Yessir." He stifled his snicker and gave him a sigh instead. "I just need a break with all the—shit that went down."

He almost allowed himself to talk like a woman. *Who the fuck blames memories for a lack of future? Certainly not any warrior from the Brotherhood.*

But it had been *part* of the reason. The fact that Shayla took up with another Team Guy on Team 4 didn't help things at all. It was a hell of a thing to come back from deployment and find someone else in your brand new king-sized bed that hit your credit card while you were sleeping in a sandy cave overseas.

So here he was, pumping iron and trying to fit in. Except that the guys on Kyle's team looked like they were right out of high school. At thirty-four years of age, he'd winced when they'd called him "Grandpa." He was part of an exclusive club. Only ten other guys on Team 3 were over thirty.

Well, he planned to show them he could probably bench press more than anyone and had taken probably a thousand more HALO jumps in his career. He would make it to fifteen years, two years from now. Then he'd see if he had the stones to stay in a full twenty, although sitting behind a desk never really appealed to him. Older guys who became too senior didn't do the active deployments. Right about ten years, most of them started moving on to something else, if they didn't do it at six.

But one thing defined Trace; he was stubborn. He'd leave on his own terms, as long as his body didn't give out on him. Every jump had his LPOs holding their breath, even though he felt fine. They'd give a younger guy time to heal if something happened. Not a thirteen-year man. And it gnawed at him that some might consider him fragile. He wanted to bust something up.

Just in time, Team 3's tall medic, Calvin Cooper, entered with a short ugly dude they called Fredo. They were about as opposite as friends could be, but word had it that they were tighter than the ass on a chipmunk. Fredo kind of looked like a small furry creature himself, with his unibrow and a wide, flat nose like an Ewok. These guys were seniors, he was told. He should show them the respect they deserved. They had a few years less service, but they were well-thought-of, and if they liked you, you were in with the rest of the squad.

"Hey, Gramps. You take your Metamucil this morning?" the shorter one asked him. Fredo's accent was all LA barrio.

"No time. I was doing the tat artist, and she took her time with me, too." He wiggled his eyebrows at Coop. He'd received intel Coop had been sweet on the little lady with tits the size of balloons. He'd let her do the frog prints up his right arm, like all the rest of the guys on Kyle's team. He pleasantly recalled how Daisy liked to smooth those knotted nipples against his bicep, and it softened his irritation at Fredo's jab about his age. So he focused on the medic.

Coop didn't react, but Trace could almost hear the cracking of granite inside the tall SEAL's chest. So Trace had to rub it in and displayed his arm, still with the plastic wrap attached, showing off his new, reddened frog print tattoo.

Fredo swore in Spanish. "He's a clown, this one. Coop, we're gonna have to watch out for him." Coop still said nothing. Fredo continued, "Besides, you're a fuckin' liar. She wouldn't want anything to do with the likes of you. She's got herself a homicide detective who brings his own cuffs. Right, Coop?"

"That's right. I still got the scars," Coop said, fingering his wrist.

Trace stood up so they could see he was nearly as tall as Coop, who was the tallest man on the squad.

"You're right, fellas. She only gave me a blowjob."

Coop smirked and still didn't rise to the bait. Fredo did it for him.

"You gotta dirty mouth, Bennett. You better hope you pack your own chute from now on."

Trace ignored the comment and continued his workout. He vowed to find a training buddy, or they'd assign him to someone who would be annoying.

"I'll spot you if you trust me," Coop said in his soft Midwest drawl.

Trace thought about it for a minute and nodded, rolled on his back and under the bar he'd set at one hundred pounds. He gripped the cool metal and extended.

"Hold it right there for ten seconds," yelled Coop.

Trace was fine until the slow count of twelve, but he wouldn't give up. Coop waited until thirteen to say ten, and Trace lowered the bar. Coop took it from him and set it gently on the bar catcher.

"That was a nice one, Trace. You're one strong motherfucker," said Coop.

"Guess you won't be calling me 'grandpa' again, then?" Trace said as he lifted the bar a second time, holding it straight-armed to a genuine ten-count, and brought it back down, where Coop rested it.

"That's a function of age, not strength. But hell, if you got it, you'll earn your spot here fair and square," added Fredo.

The beautiful Thai owner of Gunny's Gym, Amornpan, wafted back into the room, a faint scent of jasmine trailing behind her and mixing with the stink of rusty metal and hot sweat.

"Hello, fellas. You got a new guy with you?" she asked brightly.

"Yes, ma'am," Trace said as he sat up. "I'm Trace Bennett. On Kyle's squad."

"Oh, you don't have to tell me that." She slapped her forearm to show she'd noticed his tat. She put her glasses on and started working on the computer. "I'll have some paperwork for you when you're done, Mr. Bennett," she added without looking at him.

They went through several routines, and the three of them worked together nicely. Afterward, Fredo poured cold water on a towel and wore it like a hoodie. Coop's face was bright red. Trace had worked a bit longer and harder than he'd intended, but he wanted to impress the stalwarts of the team.

"So we got a vacation coming up. You up for a little sun and fun?" Coop asked him.

"Not sure what you mean. I just got here. Nothing wrong with San Diego's sun and fun."

"Nah, man. I mean Hawaii." Coop had his towel around his neck, sweat rolling down in rivulets all over his face and chest. "Bunch of us are going in on a big house on Kauai with like eight bedrooms. Got it for the week. We're bringing wives and girlfriends, so you're welcome to if you want. We're asking everyone for five hundred, and that will include everything but the bar tab, eating out, and the air fare, of course."

"Sounds good."

"Put you down for one or two?" asked Fredo.

"Just one. I'm solo right now."

"Okay, you'll probably get the couch, then." Coop continued, "Fair warning, there are a few babies coming, but no kids. Some have babies they can't be separated from yet. You get the idea."

"Yeah. Breastfeeding."

Fredo burst out laughing. "You're all right, Trace! He comes already packaged for the program."

"You gotta understand, this isn't my first picnic, and I've been on Team vacations before. I know the drill." Trace didn't want to dwell too much on some of the trips he and Shayla had taken in the past. There was a lot of naughtiness, some that got couples in trouble, and of course a whole lot of drinking. This time, he was single and kind of looking forward to it.

CHAPTER 2

GRETCHEN HAD ALL three girls in the kitchen for a quick bowl of soup before their father's girlfriend made the pickup. Clover, her teenager and oldest of the three, displayed a long face and lack of enthusiasm for anything, wearing her backpack slipping off one shoulder. She finally dumped it on the ground and climbed the stool, hovering over her soup.

"So, Mom, you going to get a bikini?" asked Rebecca. She started to pick the chicken in the chicken noodle soup from her braces.

"What makes you think I don't already have one?" Gretchen answered with a quick smile. "Or, maybe I'll go to the nude beach. What do you think about that?"

"Dumb," moaned Clover. "Nobody looks good with all their clothes off. Who wants to see all the veins and flabby butts and boobs that hang to their waist?" She blew on her soup and slurped without looking up.

Rebecca and Angie giggled. "Oh. My. God. She said

flabby butts," repeated Angie, and the two younger daughters snickered again.

"Well, these aren't your grandparents, you know." Gretchen was going to continue, but Rebecca cut right across her.

"Gramma's boobies are flat as pancakes, and she has to scoop them up like biscuit dough to put them in her bra and nearly falls over doing it."

The girls laughed again.

"Shut up, you guys. That's not nice. Gramma can't help it. That's why I'm not ever going to have any children. I want to be skinny and tall and have nothing that gives me a black eye when I run, like boobs." Clover droned on. Her little sisters thought she was hilarious.

"Okay, now, let me explain a couple of things first." Gretchen was entertained, but knew she had to give them a primer or the week-long stay with their dad and his new fiancée would turn out to be a disaster and perhaps ruin her trip. She didn't want to get midnight calls from the girls in tears and knew it was a distinct possibility.

"Give them their space," mimicked Rebecca.

"Tell Joanie her cooking is fabulous," mirrored Angela.

"Try not to listen when they start screwing and you hear Dad grunting like a pig," said Clover.

Gretchen had to smile at that one. She couldn't help but add her dose of humor. "Are you sure that's your dad you're hearing?"

"Oh, Mom! I'm gonna tell!" teased Rebecca.

"You'll do nothing of the kind," quipped Gretchen.

Listening to the girls banter and tease each other, she was proud of the way they'd turned out. They had a healthy respect for relationships and took the breakup of their parents in style, all of them knowing full well their father had been on TV. They'd even seen the video posted by one of those celebrity shows of their father doing Jell-O shots without his shirt on, lapping them up between the dancer's enormous boobs. Gretchen explained that men went crazy for boobs, that they could be led around by the nose with the chance to just look at a woman's enormous boobs, and that their father was no different.

Playing for the Portland Trailblazers was something he did. Unlike the effect he had on everyone else around him, to the girls, he was just Dad, who had a weakness for bad behavior and pretty blonde ladies much younger than he. He was special only because he was their father, not due to anything he did on the court or in the bedroom.

Gretchen hadn't accepted a penny of Tony Sanders' money. She allowed him to set up college funds for the girls, but she wanted him to feel as useless to their upbringing as she did the night she watched the video of him in her living room. Another nasty part of their breakup she kept from them is the fact that he'd hit Gretchen on two occasions. The second assault was the real reason she left. The girls didn't need to know this until they were old enough to understand.

The doorbell rang.

"Okay, it's show time!" Gretchen spouted. "Now is the time to go for a quick pee if you need to."

"Mom, they have bathrooms at the arena," said Clover. She opened the front door before Gretchen could answer.

Joanie could have made toothpaste commercials. Her dazzling white, perfectly straight teeth matched the whites of her enormous blue eyes. She had flawless, tanned skin with an eternal rosy glow to her cheeks. Angela had asked Gretchen once why her cheeks sparkled, and she had to explain Joanie wore blush. Her lips were extra full and plump, and the rosy color matched her blush.

"Hi there, girls!" Joanie exclaimed as she jumped up and down like a cheerleader. "We're going to have such a wonderful time! I can hardly wait to have pool fights and pajama parties and ice cream sundaes with you guys, so we can do some real girl talk and get to know each other!"

The enthusiasm Joanie expended was not returned.

All the basketballs on this court were half-deflated. The two younger girls looked up to their tall sister, who towered about four inches over Joanie. "Yeah. That sounds great, doesn't it?" Clover said, glancing back down on them.

The two little ones nodded obediently.

While Joanie was getting pumped up, picking up backpacks and duffel bags of things, Clover rolled her eyes at Gretchen and then put her finger down her throat, careful not to let anyone else see the action.

Gretchen frowned and then grabbed Clover and gave her a hug and kiss on the cheek. "You take good care of your two sisters, Clover. I'm putting all my faith in you," she whispered in her ear.

"I'm only doing this for you, Mom, so you can take a vacation that you sorely need. I hope you wear that bikini, and you meet a nice Hawaiian boy who," she wiggled her eyebrows and leaned in, "you know, treats you fine."

Gretchen laughed and hugged her again.

"Joanie, they've been really looking forward to spending some time with you and Tony. Thank you for doing this. You sure it's not too much?"

"Oh no!" Joanie wrinkled her perfect unlined brow. "Growing up I was always the one who took care of all the pets. We had chickens, too, and three dogs and a parakeet named Scooter. I love taking care of children and animals. I'm really good with them. You'll see, huh, girls?" She kneeled down like a coach encouraging her scrappy team, held up her palm, and gave the little ones a high five. Clover waited and fist-bumped.

Gretchen watched them all trudge down the stairs to Joanie's SUV. She pranced around the vehicle, opened up the hatch and the doors, helped to load the duffel bags wearing her pink running suit and matching pink shoes. Her ponytail, held with a pink scrunchie with a pink flower at the end, wagged from side to side as she bounced, her chest also in motion. Gretchen could only imagine the fantasies Tony must have watching her do anything.

Well, good for him. That was never me.

Joanie bounded up the steps and gave her a hug, which nearly threw her off balance. "Now. You go away and have yourself one heck of a time, and don't you worry about a thing."

Gretchen hugged her back and nearly sneezed from the heavy perfume she wore. "Thanks, Joanie. I appreciate this. You call me if anything comes up. Don't be afraid. You won't spoil my vacation," she lied.

"Nonsense. What could come up?"

Her eternal smile and peppy face bounced with the rest of her body back down the stairs, where she perched herself behind the wheel, waved, and began to roll out the driveway.

Gretchen saw the three faces of the precious joys of her life framed by the SUV windows and missed them already. As they waved, they looked sad, but Gretchen worked on herself to blow kisses and pretend she didn't have a care in the world.

But the truth was, she'd never known anything except being their mother. Playing a single woman on her own, even if it was for one week, seemed so far from her comfort zone she almost called the car back and changed her mind.

But a promise was a promise. She'd promised Kate she'd go and help her with their toddler, Grady. She also looked forward to hanging out with Tyler's sister, the famous romance novelist Linda Gray, who was also single and about Gretchen's age. If she lived her life anything close to how she wrote her books, she sounded like she'd be a whole lot of fun.

And there were to be some unattached SEALs floating through here and there, Tyler had told her. What could be wrong with that, even if they were all too young for her? Wasn't like she'd be searching for a long-term relationship, especially with those boy scouts. But a little dancing, some stargazing, and lying out on a white, sandy beach was just what the doctor ordered.

CHAPTER 3

TRACE PICKED UP his nylon duty bag, this time filled with flippers, snorkel, sunscreen, shorts, several pairs of flip flops, some tees, his TRX for workouts, and his special protein shakes and meal replacement bottles. The thing weighed nearly as much as when it was filled with firepower.

The Lihue airport on Kauai was muggy. As he set down his bag, scanning the crowd, he found Tyler Gray standing nearby. Kate was holding their new baby, about six months old, sleeping against her chest. He saw a couple other Team Guys and some SEAL froglettes, but his eye was drawn to a woman wearing a bright red flowered top and a red sun hat, unloading red suitcases with white hearts all over them. He turned to Tyler.

"Who's the eccentric with the red shit?"

Tyler grinned and glanced at his wife before answering. "My sister."

Trace took a step backward. "Next you're gonna tell me she's a drag queen. Didn't know you had that in your family tree, my man."

"Look, Grandpa. I'll bet my sister could teach even old, crusty, and arthritic you a thing or two about sex. She writes some of the hottest romance novels on the planet."

"Ew. That's a sort of tummy twister, Tyler. Reading sex scenes your sister writes?" Trace worked his face into a prune until he saw an attractive blonde in pastel colors standing behind Kate, her hand over her mouth, snickering. He softened his reaction, stood straight, and instinctively stuck out his chest.

She looked a lot like Kate, Tyler's wife.

"I'll have you know one of those books of hers is the reason Kate and I got together. I was reading it on the plane when we met. I read it to help her with technical stuff and…" Tyler hesitated.

Kate pulled out the book and showed Trace. The model on the cover was nearly naked, the veins below his belly button disappearing dangerously into the waistband of a low-hung set of well-worn jeans. He couldn't see anything of the model's face, except the chin, but there was no mistaking the dimple there, identical to Tyler's.

"You're kiddin'."

"That's my man. One hunky cover model,"

quipped Kate. She wrapped her arm around Tyler's waist, looked up, and accepted his kiss.

Trace was going to swear, but stopped himself. The blonde was still giggling.

"And I suppose you like this sort of thing?" Trace said to her.

"I love it. I love her books. Here she comes. Let me introduce her," she said.

Trace turned around, but he smelled the red woman before he got his eyes on her. She was giving instructions to an island-looking baggage handler, rummaging in her purse for some tip money. No less than four bags, all big ones precariously perched on the handler's tiny cart.

Trace checked back with Tyler, who nodded. "Hey, sis, I have a friend I want you to meet."

The lady in red glanced up and took in Trace like she'd just been given an icy glass of water on a hot day.

"Well, hello there, gorgeous!" she gushed. She stepped back, nearly collapsing the pile of suitcases on the short Hawaiian helper.

Taking a long pull from her eyes, Trace felt physically undressed as she worked her way up from his ankles, weaving as her gaze traveled up his torso and back to his face. He blushed in spite of himself.

"Oh. My. Gawd. He's shy!"

Tyler and Kate laughed out loud. The blonde woman to his left again covered her mouth with her hand and looked down.

He saw the novelist step toward him again. He raised his hands to give up when she leaned in and whispered in her throaty voice, "But something tells me you're not in the bedroom. You see sex as a full contact sport. Am I right?"

A small crowd had gathered to watch their interchange, and Trace had to do something quick or he'd just need to leave. He grabbed her around her waist, drew her to his chest, and put a lip-lock on her worthy of an airtight space seal. He growled and then whispered back to the shaking woman, "How was that? Honey, best wear your gator repellent and a bullet proof vest when playing with me."

As he released her, she wobbled, braced herself on her brother, repositioned her red sun hat, which had gotten dislodged, and sucked in air.

"So, Trace, this is my sister, Linda. I can see you've already gotten intimately acquainted with the insides of her mouth."

Trace extended his hand, which dwarfed the tiny, white, red polish adorned hand of the writer when she placed her hand there before he wrapped his fingers around it and squeezed gently.

"Very nice to meet you, romance writer Linda. I've never met one before."

Now it was her turn to blush. He could tell she wasn't used to being upstaged when it came to being outrageous. He angled his head to check out the reaction on the blonde.

Her curly hair was unruly from the long plane flight from San Diego and stuck out from behind her ears where her clip failed. He wondered how he'd missed seeing her amongst the passengers and then remembered Tyler and the family had flown First Class. She was a first class kind of lady.

"And you must be related to her," Trace said as he pointed to Kate.

She gave him a full smile and was quick to extend her arm. "I'm Gretchen Sanders, Kate's older sister."

Trace felt her warm fingers that weren't afraid to show strength. As they shook, she added, "I love reading Linda's novels, but rest assured, I'm no writer."

She tried to pull her hand back, and Trace thought it might be a good idea to hold onto her for a bit, leaning slightly toward her.

"You want a kiss, too?"

"No, thanks. The handshake is fine," she said as she stripped her hand from his grip, but then gave him another beautiful smile without blushing.

"I see you've met two of the single women already, Trace," said Fredo after he slapped him on the back. "You're lucky. If I'd have done that to Mia when I first met her—she's Armando's sister—he would have kicked my ass."

Tyler shrugged. "She needed it. Bad." He smirked at his sister, who now had her hands on her hips.

"Tyler Gray. That's a terrible comment."

"But I was just telling the truth," Tyler responded.

"Don't mind him. He was looking out for you, Linda. You said you wanted more hero material for your books. You just got one very close encounter with the wolfish kind," said Kate between laughs. The baby began to stir, and she bounced him and winked back at Trace.

Linda stood on her tiptoes, arched her back, and asked him, "So, if I asked you real nice-like, would you do it again?" She followed it up by batting her big brown eyes at him. He usually liked that sort of behavior on a woman. And the fact that she was up for round two definitely was in her favor. But he was distracted by the blonde.

"To be honest, I usually like my ladies in pairs. You get your friend here, Gretchen, and I'll see you two down at the water's edge this evening. How about that?"

Linda appeared mock disappointed. He checked blondie's face and saw a frown.

"Not me. I don't like to share."

Trace had the urge to go all commando on her,

which would have been a completely ridiculous idea.

Reel it in, Gramps. You're new on the team. The entertainment is over. Time to get serious.

"Okay, now that we got that out of the way, who needs help with their bags?"

Both Gretchen and several other ladies standing nearby, not with the Team, raised their hands. Linda Gray stood next to her bag boy and shrugged, turning around in a huff.

TEN OF THEIR party was present with others arriving on a later flight from LA. The Air BNB organizer had arranged to take them to the property and leave her fifteen-passenger van behind with them. Trace sat in the back seat with Fredo after helping to load the bags into the small compartment in the rear. They had a couple of red suitcases with the hearts stacked between them on the bench seat.

Linda and her new friend, Gretchen, sat with Kate and Tyler. Coop and Libby sat with a couple of other Team Guys who were also solo.

The operator was short, about as big around as she was tall, and sported a Mumu and a plastic orchid in her hair.

"A-Loo-Ha!" she said in the greeting of the islands. She waited, and the response was lackluster, so she started the engine to begin the air, but turned to face her audience behind in the bench seats.

"Okay, first, the ground rules. When you come to Hawaii, you have to answer back when you are greeted with the island greeting. And you do it this way, with gusto!" She inhaled and belted out, "A-Loo-Ha!"

Everyone in the van repeated her greeting back to her.

"Good. Glad that's settled. As you know, my husband will be bringing up your other group. So you just sit back and relax. I'll be using this little microphone"—she tapped the mouthpiece attached on top of a metal stem mounted on the dash—"to give you some details about our island on our way. It will take about forty-five minutes, unless we get traffic. Then it will be two hours."

She giggled in glee worthy of any horror show. Trace noticed how easy it was for her to break the ice.

"Okay, so anyone want to back out? The airplanes back to California are right over there." She pointed to the airport and got a ripple of laughter.

Trace put his right elbow on the pile of two suitcases covered in the white hearts and rested his head in his palm, waiting to be entertained. The novelist scanned over her shoulder and gave him a flirt, ignoring Fredo. When she'd turned away, Fredo knocked Trace's arm loose, jarring his repose.

"Don't fall asleep. The party's just begun, my

friend."

"How come your wife isn't here, Fredo?" he asked.

"We had twins three months ago. She didn't want them to fly, so she sent me on my own, to babysit all you bachelors, since Kyle's on that training in D.C."

Trace knew how it worked. If the Team Leader couldn't be there, even on a big recreational trip, then his two seconds—Cooper and Fredo—would take over, be his eyes and ears. Sometimes Armando, as well. But Fredo was responsible for making sure the bachelors behaved themselves and didn't negatively reflect on the Navy or the SEALs.

"Congratulations! Hope to meet them soon." Trace was pleased for the Latino SEAL. "Boys or girls?"

"One each."

"You're a fertile motherfucker."

"You don't know the half of it," Fredo said, his voice fading out to watch scenery.

Trace tapped his arm, and Fredo gave him attention. "Can you believe this?" Trace mouthed and then pointed to the red suitcases.

Fredo pointed to Tyler. "Sister," he mouthed.

Trace nodded. "Four suitcases." He motioned with his fingers and mouthed silently.

Fredo shrugged. He pointed to Kate's sister. He kissed his fingers at his lips and then pointed again at Gretchen.

Trace wiggled his eyebrows. A Team Guy's sister was one thing, but a SEAL wife's sister could cause a whole lot of heartache in numerous families, so it was watched very carefully. Fredo was giving his thumbs up. It was the go-ahead, not that Trace really needed it, to proceed.

"You know her?" Trace whispered.

Fredo nodded. He gave Trace the A-OK. "Golden," he mouthed. He added, swinging his arms as if holding a baby, "Three children."

Trace frowned. Then he gave an exaggerated shudder.

Fredo shook his head in disagreement. He showed three levels with his hands, indicating the three different heights, or ages, of Gretchen's girls. He also winked and kissed his fingers again, indicating they were nice girls.

Trace shrugged. He couldn't see himself dating a mother of three. He hoped there'd be some variety once they got to their place. Dating the novelist was totally out of the question, but that's what everyone was expecting, including the writer herself.

Way to step in it, Trace.

So far, things were not as uncomplicated as he'd hoped. But there were six days to go.

WHEN THE VAN turned left off the two-lane meandering highway and headed into the hills sparsely dotted with multi-million dollar homes, Trace could see that the venue they'd chosen was prime. Each house they passed became more estate-like, the gates got fancier, and the humidity and heat lessened the higher they climbed. Finally, they drove onto a lava rock driveway leading to an iron gate adorned with pineapple patterns. The shapes looked like pieces of a metal quilt. Their driver punched in numbers on the keypad outside, and the gate slid across the lava rock, which became part of a circular driveway in front of a plantation-style, pale yellow home. Though the structure was square with second story gables, the size of it made the second story dwarf in comparison. An even more generous wraparound deck nearly twenty feet deep was decorated with wooden gingerbread railings also with pineapple cut-out motif. Double glass doors were etched in a lacy pineapple design as well.

The air was cool with a slight breeze, yet the sun was shining without a cloud in the bright, azure sky. Below, green hills rolled amongst rows of plantings, farm animals, and occasional horses, which seemed out of place. Farthest away was the warm expanse of cream-colored beach and blue breakwater. The horizon was marred with several large hotel complexes and two spectacular golf courses. Trace knew that most tourists were housed below, near the golfing, shopping, and beach, but the old Hawaiians with money would seek the privacy and beauty of their hillside estates. It nearly took his breath away.

"Have you ever seen anything so beautiful?" Gretchen whispered as she appeared to his left.

"Nope. I don't think I have. Isn't what I was expecting to see here in Hawaii. Like how it must have looked a hundred years ago, if you could cut out the hotels," he answered.

"Oh. My. God," Linda exclaimed as she clasped her hands together. "This is the perfect setting for my next novel! *The Hawaiian Princess and the Navy SEAL*. Can't you just *feel* the romance budding? I see sex in an awesome master bedroom, which this place surely has, sex on a grandmother's Hawaiian quilt spread under a papaya tree, and sex on the sun-kissed beach. Can't you, Gretchen?"

Trace was amused by her outspoken and overtly sexual expressions, but he could see she'd embarrassed Gretchen, whose cheeks had turned a blotchy hot pink.

"She's a little ahead of herself, I'd say," whispered Trace to ease Gretchen's tension. "I mean, they've not met yet in her book, right? Has she even started it?"

Gretchen giggled and shook her head no. "But I understand her method is to start with the sex scene and then work her way forward and back from that big event." She gave him a dazed look and rolled her eyes, as well as her shoulders. "But I don't write books, and I've got zero imagination."

Trace knew she was wrong just by the way she said it.

"What time of the day is the sex at the beach?" Trace asked. He held his breath and let her struggle, but finally, she gave him a thoughtful answer.

"She'd say at sunset, a bright orange sunset. But for me, close to midnight with the black sky and all the stars on display. Maybe some ukulele music and an old Hawaiian woman singing in the background."

Trace was taken aback. It was the same vision he'd had. Without the Ukulele music.

"Ms. Sanders, I'd say you have a very good imagination," he whispered in her ear, squeezed her upper arm, and pushed past her to retrieve luggage from the van where the others were.

Gretchen was going to say something back to him but had gotten snagged by Linda Gray. He heard them discussing something as he put distance between them—well, Linda discussing and Gretchen listening. He turned his head around just enough to see Gretchen watching him walk away.

Now that was a good sign and way more to his liking.

CHAPTER 4

GRETCHEN AVOIDED TRACE'S eyes, but she could tell he watched her every chance he had. She'd not had that much attention since the TV reporters who hounded her after her husband's very public display of indecency. In that case, the heartless reporters even ramped it up when she was with her daughters. Clover had ran after one of them, but, thank goodness, didn't catch up with the cameraman, or they'd have had a lawsuit for sure.

Even that landed on the tabloid TV show, and her ex had the gall to call Gretchen up and ream her about not getting better control of their girls.

What an asshole.

The tabloids never got wind of Tony's real dark side. They were more interested in the sexcapades.

This kind of attention focused on her made her nipples knot, made her knees wobble a little, made her want to run her fingers through her hair and reposition her clip, leaving a wisp or two of curls lapping down the back of her neck because it made her feel wanted and desired. She knew her cheeks were flushed, and her panties were in a constant state of wet and cool, depending on if she was sitting or standing on the porch, hanging on to the pale yellow wooden pillar and marveling at the view below. She knew wood, especially painted wood, was not the way of the islands now. This house had obviously been built during the old plantation days when the monarchy was in its glory. The old Queen was gone now for nearly a hundred years, but her legacy of grace, of raising beautiful tropical flowers, and her love of singing and watching the young dancers swing their hips and call to each other with their graceful arms and hands was legendary. She herself had once been a beauty and had been an expert Polynesian dancer.

Maybe there was something to what Linda said, because the story of the Hawaiian princess and the Navy SEAL started fanning the flames of her heart, making the hairs on the back of her neck desire to be kissed.

She could tell he was staring at her and that he knew she was aware of it, too. She gave him a smile and did not dare look for his reaction. All she could do was fan herself with the folder she was holding and then take down and re-clip her hair again, for the tenth time in the past hour as they had been setting things up in the house.

They'd given her a room with Linda, one of the smaller ones, with twin beds. But she loved the privacy and the little marble-topped writing desk in front of the gabled window perfect for writing love letters, or romance novels. The flush of cool, ocean breeze was something she was looking forward to inhaling all night long as she slept.

Trace stood at the doorway and, of course, like a gentleman, would not come into the room without an invitation. She could imagine herself as the island princess and he a pirate sea captain, not daring to touch her for fear of losing his life. The tension was there, just the same in this century as it could have been way back over a hundred years ago.

"I think I've just found a prettier view. Too bad you can't see it," he said casually, in a near-whisper. But she heard every word.

Turning, she snickered at his lack of uniform, no hat tucked under his arm because he wore flip flops and shorts that came just to the tops of his knees. His well-developed calf muscles were covered with dark hair. His white V-neck tee shirt was so bright she nearly needed shades, and he had a pair of sunglasses tucked into the bottom of the V. His day-old stubble was distracting, as was the drip of sweat that trickled from under his chin and down between his collarbone to parts unknown. Part of the tee shirt had stuck to his chest and abdomen below.

He uncrossed his arms and angled his head, waiting for a response. "You think I look funny?"

She gave him a graceful smile worthy of an island princess of great lineage. "No, Trace. I was thinking about—"

"How nice it would be to go down to the beach," Linda interrupted, pushing the big, hulking SEAL aside. "Are you game, or do my stories of sex on the white sand make you itch?" She wiggled her eyebrows, oblivious to the scene she'd just crashed. "I'm in the mood for an umbrella drink and some bare bodies to gaze at." She opened her red suitcase up and pulled out a red beach bag. "I'm changing into my bikini now," she said as she removed her top and revealed a red bra with pink lipstick kisses on it.

Trace was out of there so fast Gretchen wasn't sure he even got a glimpse of the bra.

"You like?" Linda fondled the satin cups of her bra.

Gretchen laughed. "You're the only person I know who matches her luggage with her underwear. Very clever."

"You have no idea, dear. I had to hunt and hunt. But thank God for Amazon. Now they show me everything pink and red with hearts and kisses."

Gretchen watched through the window as another van pulled up to the front porch and several people piled out. Trace greeted several of the guys and was introduced to a pair of very cute twenty-somethings, and instantly, she was disappointed seeing his wide smile and ready hug.

Linda peered over her shoulder.

"Oh, Gretchen. Here I was jealous of you, since you've obviously attracted Trace's attention. And now we both have competition from those little sweet tarts."

Gretchen looked away from the window and walked to her bed. "No worries. I'm looking for a super rich investment mogul who owns his own island and only likes women over thirty."

"Good idea, Gretchen. SEAL's don't make that much, but I understand the sex is worth it." She examined her clothes, trying to pick out a combination. Most everything in her suitcase was red.

Gretchen was slightly irritated. "Is everything about sex with you?"

"Yup. Sex sells." She held up a red and pink flowered sarong and examined herself in the mirror, holding the fabric under her chin. "You like this on me?"

"How do you feel wearing it?"

"Positively like a cougar waiting to pounce. But the answer to your question is, yes, maybe. It's called the law of attraction." Her beautiful brown eyes sparkled. Gretchen knew she was about to get a lesson she hadn't asked for.

"So let's have it," Gretchen urged as she sat on the bed, rummaging through her own clothes.

"Everything is sales. We are selling each other right now."

"Come again?" She was seriously concerned for Linda's state of mind.

"We don't know each other very well. Just met today, right?"

"Yes. On the plane."

"Exactly. Tyler and Kate met on the plane. They fell in love on that plane that day, remember?"

Gretchen frowned. "Linda, I hope you haven't gotten the wrong message here."

"Oh, silly. I *love* women, but not in bed. But I love getting silly drunk with my women friends. Just the best thing in the world. The funny banter and gossip. I can tell you and I could do a serious drunk together and wind up feeling like we've been sisters our whole lives."

"You are close to Kate that way now?"

"No, silly. She has the baby, she has Tyler, and she's not the same as me temperament-wise. Now, Tyler? If he wasn't my brother, OMG, OMG, he would be so much fun. And we did have fun in high school. He helped fix me up big time."

"Not the other way around?"

"He never liked any of my slutty friends." She gave Gretchen a smirk. "His loss, if you ask me. Those girls would have treated him fine and worshiped the ground he walked on, too. But he fixed me up with tamer guys, and I got what I could out of them. I mean, drop dead gorgeous gentlemen, you know. Wouldn't touch me until they thought it was right. Nice guys. Oh man, I bolloxed them up something good."

"Bolloxed?"

"Messed with their brains. You know, stroked their ego, and then I just stroked them. I loved blowing their minds."

"And they never called you back."

Linda dropped another piece of lingerie and stared back at Gretchen. "Sadly, no. How did you know that?"

"Because I don't think men like to be chased. They like to do the hunting."

"But so do I."

"Then hunt for something else. Don't hunt a man. At least, if *I* did it, it wouldn't work. You have to just be there, and you hope that they get the message. Nice guys are worth it."

"I have no patience. But you see, that's why we're going to be great friends. You can teach me a lot about men. Have you had a lot of them?"

Gretchen looked at her hands folded in her lap. She would have to tell Linda the truth.

"I only had sex with one man, and I married him."

"Gretchen!" Linda ran over to the bed, pulled her up to standing position, and gave her a big hug. "You poor thing! Starved, absolutely starved! That's so unfair, sweetie." She touched Gretchen's chin and looked at her sorrowfully. "My heart is breaking for you, Gretchen." She actually produced tears, which Gretchen thought was miraculous.

Grabbing Linda's hands, which still held her, and pushing her away slightly, Gretchen regained her composure back. "I've been raising three beautiful daughters. I've had boyfriends, and we've done some things, you know, but no sex. I just don't want to have sex with someone I couldn't marry. I know it's crazy, but that's the way I was brought up. Or, at least, that's the way I *thought* I was."

Linda stepped back. "There's a story there," she said, pointing to Gretchen.

"Oh yes, there really is. Sometime when we're having those umbrella drinks, I'll tell you the tale my mother told me about the time Tyler and Kate decided to get married."

"Spill."

"I'm not going to right now. But Kate and I have different fathers."

"So your mother slept around."

"Linda, I'll tell you when I'm ready." Gretchen was getting irritated with her again. "But no, it wasn't anything like that. If you could get your mind out of the gutter, you might actually learn there are some really decent and cool love stories out there, and they're way more about love than sex."

Linda's eyes widened in surprise.

Gretchen made a beeline for the hallway so she could hit the restroom before she erupted into tears and ran smack into Trace Bennett's chest.

"Hold on there, darlin'" he said in that low growl while his deep blue eyes made her heart flutter. "I had no idea you wanted to dance so bad. You need to wait until I get my dancin' shoes on. These don't move."

She looked down at his toes, and they both watched him wiggle them. But during the show, he'd slipped his arms around her waist and her palms had spread out on his wet tee shirt. Her lips were close to his Adam's apple and the dark scruffiness of his jawline. And they were so very close to his lips… if she'd just raise her chin up, which she did. He whispered something soft, and she didn't dare listen because her spine had gone all tingly. If she wasn't imagining things, something was taking firm shape between them as he pressed her to him until their thighs touched through fabric.

"You smell like heaven, Gretchen. Like a starlit

night on a beach."

"I didn't think stars smelled like anything," she said as she waited and let him angle down toward her mouth. She was hungry for him, but just before he could cover her lips, the hallway filled with chatty newcomers.

"Well, I can see *some* people are deep into their vacation already," said Ollie. He was overflowing with suitcases, and he dropped one, which was quickly picked up by one of the twenty-somethings accompanying him.

Gretchen immediately pulled away, and she and Trace left a wide gap for the entourage to pass. The "twins" gave her a smile that hinted at warmth but was laced with something else. Ollie gave her a wink and sashayed between them all, one case above his head.

Trace had his hands in his shorts, checking out his wiggling toes. When their eyes finally connected, Gretchen saw the fire was still there, and her pulse quickened. When he gave her a lopsided smile and rubbed his chin, she nearly fainted.

More people were coming up the stairs. Trace gracefully hopped across the hallway to stand next to Gretchen. He bent down and whispered, "To be continued, my dear."

She watched him maneuver around suitcase-carrying, well-built men and young women as he made his way down the stairs. Gretchen retreated to the bedroom, closed the door, leaned against it, and closed her eyes.

"Well done."

She'd forgotten Linda was still in the room. With her breathing ragged and embarrassment stabbing her stomach lining with little pitchforks, she felt exposed and without defenses.

"You've got it bad, sweetie."

She knew Linda was right. But she had to attempt to show she was casual about the whole thing—if she could. "Just not used to the guy flirting with me before I'm ready. I'm way out of practice." She saw Linda nodding in response. Gretchen was proud of herself. Her comment was nearly one hundred percent truthful.

"He's a babe magnet, all right. I'll grant you that. I'm going to honor your territory."

"Linda, no need for that. I'm a big girl. Just rusty." Then she stopped herself. "Actually, that was a fib. I never was any good at it."

"Well, make sure you have a case of condoms, because I have a feeling you're going to get all the practice you need, plus a little extra for dessert. You'll do fine. He looks like he wants to lead, so let him. Holy hell, I wish I was in your shoes."

"Might make it into your book, then? Your mom

tells me you write your friends and enemies into all your books."

Linda laughed. "I do crazy wicked things with some of my friends. Make them have sex in strange places. If they only knew how sick and twisted I really am."

"That's what your mother says, too." She was hesitant to bring up the subject, but decided vacation time was perfect for baring it all. "What in the world do you say to your mom and dad? Especially since Tyler's on your covers."

"One. He's only on one cover."

"Kate has never told me she objects. She likes your books, and that's how I started reading you, from books I borrowed from her."

"Of course Kate's okay with it. It's my dad who had a hard time with what I wrote. Mom is, well, Mom."

"She's very proud of you and has told me several times. The girls want to write picture books, too."

"I forgot you know them well," Linda said. "She babysits for you now and then?"

"Yup. The girls love her. She teaches them to paint."

"Mom's certainly a free spirit. Ex hippies always turn out unusual. My parents never changed from what it sounds like they were in college."

"Well, I can't wait to read my character in one of your books. You'll tell me, then, so I don't miss it. Five minutes of infamy, since I probably won't do anything too flashy."

"Could be. Most my friends are in my books—not that they'd recognize themselves. I take a kernel of the truth and explode it into something they'd never think of. My guilty pleasure. But, if you want to share any details, I'm your gal. You sure you two have never met before?" Linda quickly slipped on a red polka dot bikini, turning her back so Gretchen could tie the spaghetti straps together at her shoulder blades.

"Just like the song, Linda."

"Who was that who sang it?" she asked.

"Beats me."

"Bryan something. Except it was a Yellow Polka Dot Bikini."

"You think they'll notice? That's the smallest thing I've seen. Mine's a one-piece."

"You're kidding?"

"I like a little tummy help after three girls."

"Yes, and my little tummy is all mine. No children to blame it on. A little lazy, I guess."

"Well, I tried. But in the end, all I wanted to be was just a good mom. Not a movie star or a celebrity, like you."

"Oh nonsense, Gretchen. You're gorgeous. And you married a celebrity, so you know what *that's* all about. What a total jerk, if you ask me."

"I didn't ask you." She had tied and re-tied the strings together and was finally satisfied the bow was straight. "There. I think that meets my high standards. And I double-tied it. If you get the sudden need to flash your boobs on the beach, just understand your top may not fall to the sand gracefully when you pull the strings." Gretchen fluttered her eyelashes for extra effect.

"You should be a romance writer," laughed Linda. "You're a natural. Flashing boobs and having things fall delicately to the sand. Oh my, what an imagination you have!"

"Don't lie to me. I have none."

"And you're not a very good liar, either."

CHAPTER 5

TRACE NOTED LINDA and Gretchen took one of the three vehicles left with the house, heading down to the Blue Water Bay Resort. He doubted they'd want to be on the beach at the hot part of the day, so figured he'd catch them in the bar later on, after the rest of the crew was situated back at the house. Kate and Libby were organizing a shopping trip to load up on staples, which was in the same center as the resort, so he planned on tagging along. Coop and Fredo were also going to come.

The resort held a Polynesian review every Sunday night, which was supposed to be quite spectacular, so he hoped he could get an informal date with Gretchen this evening, but he'd take Linda, too, if he had to. The whole house was commenting on Linda and her antics. But she was family and would be a source of entertainment in case any of them needed it. Therefore, she was always welcome.

Kyle called in and got the report they'd all arrived safely. He spoke briefly with Fredo and Cooper. Armando had a longer conversation with him, as there was a secret mission coming up that was going to involve only a handful of the guys.

Libby was anxious to get their shopping done, so she asked Trace if he was ready to go.

"Whenever you're ready, ma'am."

Libby grinned. Her tall, lanky good looks were a perfect match to her husband's six foot four frame. With Kyle not being present, it was left to Libby to keep the household organized and to serve as Mother Hen.

"You don't have to go all ma'am and such with me, sailor. Just call me Libby, or Coop's lady, or something like that. We're not too formal in our household."

"Yea, but don't get her mad, Trace. She's darned pretty when she's flustered, but wicked with the words," Coop admitted, coming from behind Libby and taking her into his arms backwards. He planted a kiss on her neck.

"Duly noted, Coop." Trace bowed to Libby. "Your chariot awaits, madame, when you are ready."

Libby turned in Coop's arms. "I like this new guy. He's not going to stay single long, I can tell. He's a charmer."

"Permission granted to flirt, Libby, but just remember who you come home with."

"Always," she whispered and kissed Coop full on the lips, standing on her tiptoes.

Kate appeared, handed the baby to Tyler, and the four of them jumped in one of the Jeeps. Trace honked the horn, and soon Fredo, who had changed his shirt into a bright red Hawaiian print, jumped in the passenger seat up front with Trace.

The large, modern grocery store was somewhat unexpected. It had a world-class deli, a fantastic selection of beers from around the world, even a sushi bar and pizza oven, as well as a full bakery. Their basket was filled with items not normally on Trace's bachelor grocery lists, but a huge variety of chips and ice cream balanced out the otherwise healthy fare. He knew he was in for some good home cooking, a luxury in his world.

"We have a signup list on the refrig," Libby told him. "Kate, Gina, and I will take turns doing the cooking, but you guys get to do prep and cleanup. We're putting the twins in charge of housekeeping." She rolled her eyes.

"Sounds like you have everything covered."

"We've done these big trips several times. They are a lot of fun, but with the sheet, no one is stuck with all the work. Did your other Team go on trips together?" she asked.

Trace always avoided thinking about his past married life and never talked about it with anyone. "I went on a couple before me and the ex parted ways. They were not run the same. Big booze parties with a lot of apologizing afterwards. I can tell you've got it dialed down."

"That's the way Christy Lansdowne runs it, like Kyle runs the team. I just watch and follow what she does. I'm sure she learned it from another SEAL wife when Kyle was first starting out."

"Good leadership all the way around. I can see why it was so difficult for me to get attached to Kyle's team. He and Christy are a great combination. We're all lucky to be on Team 3."

"I think so, too."

The bill came to over five hundred dollars, which Libby paid from an envelope of cash she carried in her purse. Fredo was in line behind them with his favorite tequila and a bag of limes.

"I can add those on here. Come on down, Fredo," said Libby.

"No, I got this." Fredo answered. Trace knew that meant the tequila would be housed in his room, not in the kitchen with all the other food and drink.

Posters advertising the Sunday night buffet and show were plastered everywhere.

Coop and Trace wheeled out the two shopping

carts, and everyone loaded up the bags in the small storage in the back of the Jeep. Trace handed the keys to Coop.

"I'm going to try to find Gretchen and Linda. Going to see if I can interest them in the show tonight. You guys going to come?"

"I'd like to," said Libby. "We can meet you there." She examined his shorts and flip-flops. "Won't you have to go home and change?"

"Honey, this is Hawaii," Coop interrupted. "Even the bankers wear flip flops and shorts, and half of them are barefoot behind the counter. He'll be fine." He took the keys. "Best of luck. You get stood up and need a ride, give me a call, hear?"

"Roger that. Thanks, Coop."

Trace searched the large open-beamed lobby and reception area at the resort then headed to the bar area and patio, which had outstanding views of the Hanalei Valley. Just as Gretchen had described, the sunset was going to be a bright orange one, judging from the glow already forming in the late afternoon horizon. Large white clouds towered in the late afternoon sky, tinged in pink, which promised a light shower by morning if the trade winds blew them ashore. Kauai was the greenest of all the Hawaiian chain, with rainfall on some of its peaks nearly the highest in the world, peppering the green volcano-created hillsides with waterfalls.

The women weren't there.

He followed a path of crushed rock down to the beach area below the resort and had no trouble spotting Linda Gray's floppy red hat. Next to her, Gretchen lay on her belly reading a book. They were shaded by a thatched palapa. Linda had been served a hollowed-out pineapple drink, while Gretchen was sipping on something pink with an umbrella and fresh fruit adorning the side of the tall glass.

Trace was surprised the beach was nearly deserted.

"Well, look who I found!" he said.

Gretchen greeted him with a warm smile as she sat up. Her oiled body glistened in the diffuse light. Linda's back and shoulders already looked like they were turning red.

"Oh, Trace. You're here just in time." Linda rummaged through her large, red beach bag. Holding up a tube of lotion, she asked, "Can you put this on my back, please?" She raised her glasses and winked at him for a special effect.

He grabbed the tube and noted she was only using a sunscreen of twenty. "You need something stronger, Linda. You're red already."

"See? I told you so," added Gretchen. "Here, use this on her." She handed him a blue spray bottle with sunscreen rated fifty.

He applied the spray, and Linda arched back with a hiss crossing her teeth. "Ouch, that's cold."

"You're a little burned. You should stay out of the sun for a day or two," he said as he smoothed the oil over her skin gently. "The sun is hotter here than in California. Need to give your body time to adjust." He turned to address Gretchen, "May I?"

"Go right ahead."

Trace removed his shirt and gave himself a spray chest side and back side, and after smoothing the foam, he used the remainder on his hands for his face and followed up with a little extra to his lower legs. When he was finished, both women were staring at him with their jaws dropping.

His immediate reaction was embarrassment, and he made a point to re-apply the sunscreen to his face to cover up a possible blush forming there.

"Anyone up for going in the water?" he asked.

Both girls stood up.

"I think you'd better wear a shirt, Linda, with your coloring," Trace added.

"Can I wear yours?" She batted her brown eyes at him.

He acquiesced, handing it to her. She slipped it over her shoulders and winked at Gretchen. That's when he noticed she had become quiet all of a sudden. "Well, ladies," he said, as he extended his elbows. "Shall we dip our toes in the surf?" They locked arms, and the threesome went down to the water's edge.

"About time we saw some nice abs and biceps," quipped Linda, holding her hat atop her head against a breeze that threatened to remove it.

"Glad I could oblige."

Gretchen was still quiet, but her arm linked through his gave him a spark of excitement at the feel of flesh on flesh.

"There's a big party tonight here," he began. "They do a Sunday night buffet and a Polynesian review. Either of you interested in attending? I think Libby and Coop and some of the others are planning on coming down."

"I saw that," whispered Gretchen. "Looks like fun. Do they actually swallow fire?"

Trace shrugged. "Beats me, but it showcases the native dances and some customs of the islands—all the islands in the South Pacific, not just the Hawaiian chain. It was recommended by our guide."

At the water, Linda insisted on getting Trace totally soaked as Gretchen hung back by herself. The novelist changed her mind and opted to return to their palapa and seek some shade, so she left Trace and Gretchen wandering down the beach.

"You having fun?"

Gretchen smiled to her toes. "I was just thinking

about that."

"That means you don't take enough vacations."

"You're spot on with that one, Trace. I've just been concentrating on being a good mom, raising the girls, and paying the bills." After a brief silence, she corrected herself. "*Not* complaining or anything. I have a nice life. And it's my job. I love being a mom, but honestly, everything else was put on hold when I became single."

"I've been told your girls are first class, like their mother."

"Well, you don't want to come around on laundry or cleaning day. I look like the Wicked Witch of the West, and my demeanor is far from pleasant. The two older girls find every excuse in the book to be gone that day."

Trace liked that she didn't take herself seriously, and he also liked the way the sounds of their combined laughter mingled together.

"How about you?" she asked. She unclipped her hair and then folded it back into place again.

"It's getting better. I wasn't so sure earlier on." He checked to make sure Linda wasn't within earshot. "Your friend here cuts a wide swath. Kind of sucks up the oxygen in the room."

"Even at the beach." Gretchen chuckled again. "But she means well. I think she's actually afraid of herself. More than she likes to let on."

"And perhaps a touch too lonely," said Trace.

Gretchen sighed at that one. "Being single for me is one thing. But for her? Why, she's supposed to be the world's expert on sex and all things romantic, but has no romantic life of her own."

"Doesn't seem fair, does it?" he asked her. The lowered sun had created a bright peach sky as the fluffy clouds morphed into what looked like big clumps of suspended cotton candy. Her honest eyes searched his, and the urge to kiss her rekindled.

"Maybe you should scratch that itch, Trace. I think she's up for a little adventure."

"Ah! Well," he admitted, "I have another lass I'm sort of interested in, if she'll give me the time of day—"

They paused, and he found it natural to take her right hand, lacing his fingers between hers. They continued sauntering down the beach, their arms swaying with their hands still locked together.

Gretchen abruptly came to a stop. "I've got six days to give you, Trace. And then, I go back to Portland and resume my motherly duties."

She said it with her laughing eyes, but the comment was serious. He moved his hands to her face, tipped her head back, and kissed her gently on her sweet lips. He loved the feeling of standing with her with the roar of the ocean at their side, her body shaking slightly.

"Don't be afraid, Gretchen. Just let yourself enjoy

what's right in front of you."

She wrapped her arms around him and buried the side of her face in his chest. But even though he stood firm, he could still feel her shaking. He could tell she needed time.

Well, the truth was he did, too.

CHAPTER 6

GRETCHEN AND LINDA sat with their crowd after the huge dinner. Several of the men had left to go get drinks in the bar, including Trace. When the lights began to dim and it was obvious the program was starting, Gretchen looked around to see if he was on his way back to her side, but as the long Hawaiian chant began and dancers took to the stage, it became clear the men had decided to view the program from the back. She still couldn't locate any of them.

No one else seemed to notice.

One by one, the performers demonstrated different costumes and themes from the various lands of the South Pacific. She watched the all-male fire dancers who did, indeed, swallow lit torches and perform acrobatics between flames, carrying wooden implements. It was a spectacular display, and soon, she forgot about the vacant seat next to her.

The stage was darkened, and then a gorgeous Polynesian dancer dressed in all white came out covered in flowers. Other young dancers spread petals all over the dance floor and kept time with the gentle sway of the most sensual hula Gretchen had ever seen.

An older, heavy-set woman sat to the side, picked up a ukulele, and began singing the beautiful Hawaiian wedding song. The dancer turned her beautiful body to the side and welcomed her male partner, also dressed in white. It didn't take Gretchen long to recognize Trace's physique. His sandy wind-blown hair and bright smile was a welcome sight. He wore white long pants and a white shirt, unbuttoned, not leaving much to the imagination. Gretchen saw the audience react to his ripped upper torso. He was also barefoot. He smiled to the audience and took a short bow to the maiden.

The crowd loved it. They whistled and clapped, recognizing that he'd been picked from the guests to dance with this lovely maiden. She undulated in front of him and then at his side. Try as he might, he couldn't keep up with her, but made a good effort. She drifted to his front and pulled his shirt back over his shoulders and dropped it on the stage, revealing Trace's huge shoulders, his long muscular arms, and the way his hips swung from side to side, which delighted the female part of the audience.

The dancer smiled demurely, moved herself in

front of him, and wrapped his arms around her as they inched first to the right and then to the left together. She pulled away and took one of the flowers from her hair and placed it behind his ear, kissing his cheek.

She demonstrated how fast her hips could swivel, something Trace could not duplicate or even come close to doing.

Soon, Coop, Armando, and a couple other SEALs appeared at the rear of the stage, all shirtless, all attempting to follow the beautiful apparition in white as she moved from man to man, teasing them.

Gretchen knew the normal men they chose from the audiences were overweight, sunburned senior citizens or guys who wouldn't take their dark socks off. Tonight, the audience was lucky to have some actual men of steel front and center, demonstrating hours of PT and training, most of them better developed than the male dancers in the review. Young girls ran up to the stage and threw their leis at the men, who allowed themselves to be "captured" by the flower lassos.

The older woman drew her song to an end as the beautiful dancer cuddled in Trace's arms again to close the program. But instead of taking her in his arms, Trace jumped from the stage and came running through the aisle. Within seconds, he appeared, hoisted Gretchen from her seat, and carried her off down the beach.

Her heart thumped as she watched the excited crowd over his shoulder. Cheers and clapping erupted and then faded as Trace carried her away into the shadows. He let her slide down his front side. She didn't back away from him as he wrapped his arms around her waist, crossing her wrists behind his neck and then running her fingers through his hair.

"Thought you wouldn't mind a little adventure. Thanks for being a good sport," he whispered. Then he kissed her.

Her body was in flames at the touch of his mouth on hers as he kissed down her neck and under her ear. She didn't shy away as his groin pressed against her. But she had to whimper as his hand slipped under her blouse, smoothed over the small of her back, and then slid to her front side, where he slowly drew one hand up to cover her breast.

She needed air, gasping at his squeeze. He watched her intently and then kissed her just as her involuntary moan pierced the sounds of the sea when his thumb and forefinger pinched her nipple.

He pressed against her again, and this time, she raised her leg, feeling his hip and muscled thigh against her own.

His beautiful, chiseled body shone perfectly in the moonlight like a Greek statue. Her fingers splayed to travel the hardness of his midsection, up over his pecs, and then back down again. His hand guided hers to his length, bursting against the fabric of the white, stretchy pants.

He slipped his palm under her sarong, feeling the length of her upper leg and then traveling to her butt, pulling her into him deeper. Her fingers lingered on the zipper of his pants as her pubic bone rode his thigh, cresting waves of pleasure all over her body.

He lifted her, and she wrapped her legs around his waist. She tasted the saltiness of his chest, listened to his heartbeat, and flicked her tongue over his nipple, which returned a satisfying groan back to her.

She was oblivious to everything else. The ocean waves cresting and breaking along the wet sand mimicked the beat of her heart. His breathing was ragged, his kisses desperately deep and getting harder. Somewhere hid thoughts about privacy and decorum, but she'd shed them, just as she now shed her skirt. He kneeled in front of her and took her panties down with his teeth, which made her whole body shake with need. His tongue found her slit, and she gasped, clutching him tighter, pulling her shirt up to release her breasts.

She lowered herself to her knees, tasting the sour saltiness of her own arousal on his lips and tongue. Her fingers felt for his zipper, which he'd already undone. Her knees hugged his hips as he leaned back. Their fingers laced together, guiding his cock to her opening until his full penetration with a sigh coming from both of them. He held her hips and pressed her down on him so that he nestled deep, and she nearly passed out.

It had been years since she'd been desired, since she'd felt these flames now consuming her. It had been too long, and now, she was quickly losing control, begging him to take her hard and without any hesitation. She met his thrusts with her own pressure, her internal muscles welcoming him to her womanhood. Her kisses showered his ears, eyes, and the top of his head as his teeth and tongue devoured and suckled her breasts.

She had no idea she had felt such emptiness, now filled with his glorious length. Aware that she was totally wanton, Gretchen asked for more. He flipped her body, gently laying her back on the wild grasses under the palm. He thrust deep and hard, and she held him there, squeezing and pressing his groin into her. His hips moved fluidly, pumping her wildly as if testing how much she could take. All she knew was that she wanted more, had always needed more, and would need more than this quick little tryst in the moonlight dangerously stolen on this magical evening under the stars.

Years of loneliness withered away as their lovemaking turned her bones to rubber and opened up the deep chasm of her soul. Whoever he was, no matter what was to follow next, Trace had brought her from the dead to the living, showing her that it had all been worth it. It mattered not how long it lasted. She'd been found, touched by a man in ways she never knew possible.

She'd be powerless to stop it now. She would forever remain awakened.

CHAPTER 7

HE SQUEEZED HER hand so hard on their walk back to the venue she had to remind him to release her fingers. But she smiled as she said it, and he told her he was sorry if he'd hurt her.

"Don't want to let you go."

"I like that," she admitted.

Her thigh brushed against his as they approached their group. Her clip had been lost, and her blonde hair was everywhere about her shoulders, framing her pretty face, her flushed cheeks, and plump lips he'd not had nearly enough time to explore. His breath had barely returned to normal, but his heartbeat was still rapid, matching her pulse. Her scent had charmed him, making him feel wild with need all over again. If she'd let him, he'd not let her sleep a minute of their time together.

Linda, of course, picked up on the change in their demeanor. He stood before her not ashamed of a thing.

The writer's eyes glistened as she was nearly brought to tears. Gretchen leaned against him, and he put his hands possessively on her upper arms, rubbing up and down, wishing he could feel her smooth skin under the blouse. His member was pressing already against her rear.

"Hey, your bride-to-be was left without a groom on stage, my man," shouted Fredo when he saw him. "Don't you know you're not supposed to leave a woman at the altar?"

He didn't care. They could rib him from now until the flight home. He was the happiest he'd been in two years, at least.

"Where's your shirt, Romeo?" Armando asked him. He too winked at Gretchen. "That was quite a performance, Trace. Way to make a lasting impression on your brothers' wives!"

Trace realized he had to return the white pants and get back his own clothes and flip-flops. Gretchen was working with her hair and tucking it in to make an attractive French twist without her clip. Her cheeks were still pink.

"I have to get my stuff behind stage. Wait for me here," he whispered.

Trace received praise from the pretty dancers who flirted with him, begging him to return tomorrow night. He politely declined. He was handed his clothes in a big plastic bag and shown to the dressing room to change.

When Trace returned to the group, everyone had decided to retire to the bar area. He wrapped his arm around Gretchen's shoulders and sat for a bit, enjoying the relaxed banter and laughter. More than once, he was called out for his dancing skills.

"You should see Amornpan dance, Trace. Gunny left her the gym when he passed," Fredo whispered.

"Really? I did wonder about the name."

"Sanouk is their son."

"I've seen him. Tall kid."

"Yeah, he's a good kid, too. Wants to become a SEAL some day. Has grown up with all of us since he and his mother came over several years ago just before Gunny passed."

"I'm glad he got to see his son."

Fredo paused. "She teaches Thai dancing at the teen center to some of the neighborhood girls."

"Bet they love that."

"Most requested class at the Center. We've got computer classes for these kids, too. Working to keep them out of trouble. You'll have to stop by so you can get involved."

Trace had heard wonderful things about the project the men on Kyle's team had personally sponsored, using the abandoned Catholic school donated by the church.

"Count me in."

The group decided to call it an early night, so he and Gretchen went with several others in the van. Overcrowded conditions made it necessary for her to sit on his lap, which he didn't mind at all. Linda found one of the single guys to drive the Jeep back.

It became apparent the sleeping arrangements would not allow Trace and Gretchen to have any privacy.

"Maybe we can sneak off tomorrow night," she whispered to him as she kissed him good night. "Thanks so much for sweeping me off my feet."

"The pleasure was all mine, Gretchen." He was at a loss for words.

"What is it, Trace?"

"I feel like I should apologize."

"For what?"

"Well, coming on too strong. This isn't who I am. I don't want you to get a wrong impression of me."

"You?" She stood before him with her hands on her hips. "What about *my* reputation?"

"Except you know you don't have to apologize."

"Good because I'm not going to. I didn't do anything I didn't want to, Trace."

She sighed, and Trace sent her upstairs with a kiss.

He found a game of cards had started in the living

room, so he watched it deteriorate until no one could remember anything and the drink caught up to them all. One by one, the company left, giving Trace the chance to bring out his blankets and an extra pillow Libby had retrieved from one of the linen closets. He changed into his red, white, and blue pajama bottoms, left his shirt off, and tried to find a comfortable position to fall asleep in. But his feet still hung over the end of the couch, and the ceiling fan was blowing down cold air. He got up to turn the fan off when he saw Gretchen's form coming down the stairs.

"I can't sleep. How about you?" she asked.

"Same here." He looked at her sheer nightgown, which revealed just enough of her body to make her look sexy as hell. But he'd decided to slow things down a bit, to underscore what he'd said earlier. "You cold?"

"A little." She was rubbing her arms.

Trace pulled one of the blankets around them both and took them outside onto the veranda. There was no view except the stars and the moon trying to shift from behind the large clouds that threatened an early morning rain.

"I got your stars here," he whispered. Gretchen had tucked herself under his chin.

She didn't say anything for a bit so he asked her for her thoughts.

"It's like I've stepped back in time."

He felt the same way. "Those were carefree days. But, man, I was a crazy, dumb kid with no clue. Next thing I knew, I was in the Navy, puking my guts out at BUD/S, then graduating one day and getting married the next. I guess I don't do anything slow."

"Do you slow dance?"

"I do."

They started to move together to sounds of a distant singer calling to them. Her head felt warm against his bare chest. He loved the feel of her back and buttocks under the thin white fabric of her nightgown as his hand lazily traveled over the hills and valleys of this spectacular woman.

"Tell me about your husband. He was a basketball player?"

"Tony Sanders, Center for the Trailblazers."

"Oh, *that* basketball player. He's a hell of an athlete. How come a smart guy like him let you get away? That just doesn't make any sense."

"He was my first love. Maybe without all the traveling, it might have worked. But he liked to fool around, and toward the end, he turned kind of violent. I didn't want to believe it at first. And then I saw proof he'd been fooling around probably our whole marriage. You know what they say, the last to know. That was me."

"I'm sorry you had to go through all that. My ex was the same way. That sort of behavior doesn't appeal to me, although you'd never know it, based on tonight." He squeezed her waist and pressed her to him as she giggled into his chest.

"Did we really do that? Do you suppose anyone saw us?"

"I know they didn't."

"How do you know that?" she asked.

He chuckled. "Well, honestly, I don't, but I thought it sounded good." He drew her away from him and searched her face. "Does it really matter?"

"No."

He lifted her chin and kissed her. "I think it was perfect. I'd do it again in a heartbeat."

She matched his kiss, her taut nipples searing his flesh beneath her nightie. He lifted the fabric, and his fingers rubbed over the satin skin of her buttocks as she pressed her mound into his lower belly.

"Wish I had a king-sized bed."

"Me, too."

"Will the couch do if I promise to make it up to you?"

"Do you keep all your promises?"

"Always, Gretchen. You'll learn that in time."

He felt her stiffen at the suggestion of an ongoing relationship. When he brushed the backs of his fingers against her cheek, she softened when he whispered, "Or we could just stay out here all night and watch the stars."

"And you'll keep me warm?"

"Baby, I'm going to make you so hot you'll explode."

CHAPTER 8

GRETCHEN AWOKE TO the sounds of someone grinding coffee. She was naked and sweaty, lying on her side with her back to him. His arm was draped possessively over her hip, his hand gently squeezing her breast.

"Morning," he whispered in her ear.

It was the perfect start to a new, sparkling day—something she'd dreamt about for several lonely years since her breakup with Tony. Getting hot and sweaty and being whispered to by this hunk of a man first thing in the morning was the medicine she'd needed.

She slowly turned to face him, their legs entangling again, as she hugged his thigh between hers. "Morning, handsome. I'm so grateful you showed me all those wonderful dance moves. The hip action and the—"

She gasped as his fingers pinched her nipple, and he pressed her onto her back and into the couch.

"You want some coffee?" he asked after he'd taken

several deep kisses. The smell of their combined bodies made her drunk. She didn't want to wake up, but knew they'd not have privacy for very much longer.

"I'd love some."

He smirked, adjusting his muscled thighs and his other more delicate parts. Bending over, he slipped his pajama bottoms up over his hips and stood. Gretchen sat up, clutching the coverlet to her chest. She saw Coop's wife, Libby, and her sister, Kate, busying themselves with breakfast preparations and cleanup from last night's mini-party.

"Morning, ladies." He gave them a wave. The two SEAL wives nearly jumped out of their skins.

"Were you comfortable last night, Trace?" asked Kate with a wink to her sister.

"Didn't have enough room, but there were compensating factors." He walked over to the countertop and poured a cup of black coffee. "Does she like cream?" he whispered in Kate's ear, but Gretchen heard every word.

"You mean that Hawaiian princess you picked up at the show last night?" she teased.

"Yes, that one. Your beautiful sister."

She broke out into a wide smile. "She does." She cleared her throat while Trace foraged in the refrigerator. "Morning, sis," Kate shouted to her.

Gretchen answered, "Morning, Kate," from the

couch. She attempted to stand up, being careful to keep the cover wrapped around her. Her nightie was draped over a lamp across the room and wouldn't give her much privacy.

Trace studied her, his half-smile looking more sexy than he had a right to.

"I took advantage of her, I'm afraid, Kate," he whispered as they both studied Gretchen's face.

"I certainly hope so," Kate quipped in return. "Either that or she's coming down with a fever."

"You going to stand there, or do I get my coffee?" Gretchen asked.

"Absolutely, ma'am. But it appears your hands are a bit full. Not that I'd complain if you had a blanket malfunction." Trace grinned on his way over to delivering her steaming cup. "Need a little help?"

She tried to ignore him, which was impossible to do since she could feel his massive body heat through the blanket. The coffee was warm and smooth.

"Hmmm. Perfect. Perfect start to a new day," she whispered to his tanned face just before she placed a soft kiss on his hungry lips.

"Don't get me started."

She smiled up at him again, took another sip, and traced his mouth with her forefinger. "I didn't think you ever stopped."

"You've only known me for—what?—a few hours,

and already you have me pegged. Good job."

"Trace." She placed her forefinger into his chest. "You might think you're a mysterious superhero, but I've got your number."

He showed her his wrists like he expected she'd cuff him. "Beam me up. I'm all yours. You can ring my number all day"—he leaned in to whisper directly into her ear again—"and please, please, all night. I'll be your slave. I take instruction well."

Those words sent a zinger down her spine. She couldn't look at him, so focused on his heavy breathing and how his maleness enveloped her in warm sunshine.

"You want your nightie? That see-through thing that drove me wild last night?"

There was no mistaking the bulge building in his red, white, and blue pajama bottoms.

"Please."

She watched his bare back as he made his way over to the lamp. Kate and Libby were transfixed. Her sister's eyes were the size of saucers.

Trace wrapped the nightgown around his neck like a scarf and returned. "Take it off me," he said with a wink.

Gretchen had to address their audience, so changed the subject. "Coffee's good, ladies."

Libby approached and said quickly, "We're about

to have a whole room full of people here in just a few minutes." She grabbed Gretchen's nightgown and handed it back to her. "Why don't you two take a shower before all the hot water is gone? The twins are not up yet, so now's your chance. Trust me on this. I've traveled with them before."

Gretchen donned her gown quickly and helped Trace fold the bedding and tuck it into the hall closet. They climbed the stairs together, but found the sole bathroom door locked.

"I'll be out in a minute," Linda said behind the door. They could hear sounds of a shower.

"Trace, you go downstairs and use the other one. I'll wait until Linda's done. I'll meet you back down there for breakfast, okay?"

He reluctantly agreed. She knew if she let him, they'd have spent an hour fooling around and would miss breakfast entirely.

Not that it was a bad idea. But Gretchen felt like it was time to come up for air and start living in the real world.

TRACE WORRIED AS he listened to Gretchen take a call from her oldest daughter. Everyone stopped eating and watched her happy expression turn from distress to outright fear and panic. Whatever was being communicated, it wasn't good. He could barely hear the sobbing pleas for help.

"Clover, calm down. How did this happen?"

He could not make out all the words until he caught Clover's words, "Three men showed up at the school while I was waiting for Joanie after practice, and they took me in a van."

Kate flew to Gretchen's side, holding the sleeping baby. The two sisters stared at each other in shock.

"Do they have all three of you?"

"No. Angela and Becky are with Gramma."

Although Gretchen let out a sigh of relief, she was still very pale, and Trace thought she might faint. Then he heard a man's voice come on the line. Trace grabbed the phone from her hands. Gretchen fell into Kate's arms, and the baby awoke, startled.

"—And we have your oldest daughter. She is safe at the moment," the man said in heavily accented Spanish, "and if you cooperate, all will end well."

"Who the fuck is this?" Trace ranted to the phone.

"Ah, Señor, not necessary to use profanity. This only makes the Indians restless and we're trying to conduct business here with Mrs. Sanders. You are her spokesperson?"

"Trace Bennett."

"You are a friend of the family, Trace Bennett? Please put Mrs. Sanders back on the phone. With all due respect, señor."

Everyone sitting at the large dining table stared at the three of them. Tyler took the squirming baby from Kate. Linda put her arm around Gretchen and kneeled at her side. Trace covered the mouthpiece and informed them, "They have Gretchen's daughter."

The room erupted in soft curses. Cooper stood and placed his phone to his ear. Trace assumed he was calling Kyle, who was still in Washington, D.C. Others called home to check on the safety of their own families and to alert the Team network. Gretchen was part of the SEAL community and would get their complete support. Though she lived in Portland, he knew it would be arranged that other members of the community would stay with her and give aid if necessary.

"Señor? I would like to speak to Mrs. Sanders, please," the voice repeated.

Gretchen extricated herself from Kate's embrace and reached for the phone, trying to grab it from Trace's fingers. He held it just out of reach. Finally, she scolded him. "I need to talk to her, Trace. Give it to me right now!"

He handed the phone back. His blood boiled, and he struggled with the urge to rip the kidnapper's arms off while he tore the creep's jugular open with his bare teeth. On his feet, he started pacing and thinking, clenching and unclenching his fists. He was waiting for the cloud of emotions to subside and the clarity of a plan to emerge, but didn't yet find any comfort or path. There were too many details he needed to ascertain. Coop had just finished his call and quietly appeared beside him.

"We get that number and I'll give it to my NSA contact, Trace," he whispered.

"Thanks, man."

"Where are they?" Coop asked.

"I'm thinking Portland, but not sure."

Gretchen was still listening to instructions. "H-how much of a *little* compensation is *little?*" Gretchen said bitterly, waiting for a response. "But I'm in Hawaii." She was flustered, stammering. "I have to call my ex-husband. Where have you taken her?"

Trace gently gripped her arm, adjusting her wrist and hand to expose the phone number on the phone screen for Coop then pushed "Speaker" so the whole room could hear the conversation. He double-checked with her first, gave her a peck on the cheek, and she nodded her approval. Coop jotted a note and got back on his own phone.

The speaker crackled and squawked, "Like I said, Mrs. Sanders, she is safe and being watched over. She is being fed and given water, so no need to be concerned."

Gretchen sucked in a breath and boomed right back at the man, "You fuckin' better take very good care of my daughter, you animal!"

Trace was astounded.

The voice on the other end of the phone sighed. "Mrs. Sanders, like I told your friend, the use of profanity is not necessary. It is not our intention to hurt your daughter, Mrs. Sanders. We are looking for just our little transaction fee, and then we will be out of your hair. Your beautiful daughter will be returned to you unharmed and untouched. I give you my word."

Gretchen's body tensed as several Team members and their wives swore under their breath and whispered amongst themselves. Trace could see already a plan was being formulated. The distance was a factor, but they were used to four plus hour flights to an op.

Coop whispered to Trace, "Okay, I'm having the phone number traced. You want Libby to get you and Gretchen to Portland? She checked, and there's a direct flight at noon you might be able to catch."

"Thanks, I think that would be a good idea. I'll pay you back."

"Not a problem. We can tag along, too, if you want us to."

"You got the ladies here, Coop. Not fair to have you do this."

"No, Trace. You don't understand. Maybe it was different on Team 8, but on *this* team, we stick together. If you think we're in the way, we'll not do it. But I don't think it's asking or expecting too much. You'd do the same for me; I know you would."

Trace nodded and gave a brief smile to Libby, who got on her cell phone immediately.

Gretchen's voice was getting shaky, and Trace could tell her emotions were confusing her. "I asked you before, how much? How much for my daughter?"

The voice paused. "One million dollars."

It might as well have been ten million. Trace suspected this would be an impossible figure to come up with. The room was once again filled with whispered profanity. Gretchen's breathing was irregular, her chest shaking with each inhale and exhale. He helped her put the phone down on the table and then folded her in his arms while they listened to the sole voice on the other end of the line through the speaker.

"I will give you one more chance to speak with your daughter, and then we will sign off for now. No tricks, please, Mrs. Sanders. You must keep the girl calm so I don't have to sedate her."

Gretchen leaned over the table and shouted into the phone's speaker, "Don't you fuckin' touch a hair on her body! Let me speak to my daughter now!" She braced her weight with her palms on the table, took a deep breath, and closed her eyes. Just as she was about done with her exhale, she heard her daughter's voice.

"Mom?" Clover's weak voice broke Trace's heart.

"I'm scared."

"Did they hurt you, sweetie?" Gretchen asked.

"No. But they're creepy." Clover sobbed and then sniffled. In a whisper, she said, "Mom, I'm in my *spandex*." Her voice trailed off.

Trace didn't understand at first what she was saying.

"Didn't you bring your warm-up suit?"

"Just the jacket, and it's cold in here."

Gretchen was holding herself together now, trying to give comfort to Clover. "I know, sweetie. Ask them for a blanket or something to wrap around your legs. You have to stay warm, and be sure to drink water."

"When are you coming to get me?"

It was the question that hung in the air nobody had an answer for.

"As soon as I can. I have to get hold of your dad. Have they tried calling him?"

"Yes. He doesn't pick up."

Gretchen gritted her teeth. "How did this happen, Clover?"

"I was waiting for Joanie. She was late. Everyone just left me, Mom." She wavered and soon began to sob again. "I'm scared, Mom."

The phone made muffled sounds, and then the male voice came on the line again. "So this is how it's going to happen," he began.

Gretchen interrupted him. "No, you don't understand. I can't do anything until I get in touch with Clover's father. He's the one in town, and he's the only one who can arrange that kind of money. So you're going to have to wait. I'm just telling the truth of how it is. I wish it was different, but you're going to have to give us some time to get this figured out."

Trace noticed she got stronger the longer she spoke.

"I do understand, Mrs. Sanders. I'm willing to be flexible, within reason. But don't take too long."

"You need to keep calling him. And I think Clover has his girlfriend's number with her somewhere, too."

"Okay. I am a very patient man, Mrs. Sanders. We will continue to try getting through to him, and we will call you back."

"I'm going to take the first flight home." She looked at Libby who nodded her head. "But I'll have my friends keep trying Tony as well."

"Very well. One other thing, you are not to involve the police. Trust me when I say that things will not go well for your lovely daughter, Clover. Such a special child. It would be a shame—"

Trace had the urge to grab the phone from Gretchen again to give the guy a piece of his mind, but Gretchen beat him to it.

"You have no idea who you're dealing with. Like I

said before, you harm one hair on her body and if it's the last thing I do, if it takes my whole life, I'll find you and your little cadre of demons and I will personally excise you from this planet. That's not a threat. That's a fact!" Gretchen's face was red with anger.

The gentleman on the phone laughed softly. But then they could hear Clover's outburst in the background, echoing in a large space, like a warehouse or hangar, "Don't touch me!"

The voice continued. "I can see where she gets her spirit. I hope, for her sake, it is not in vain. We'll be in touch."

The phone went dead.

CHAPTER 9

THE WOMEN CAME over to help Gretchen take a place on the couch. Linda brought her a tall glass of ice water. Several hands lifted her legs and massaged her feet while Kate massaged her shoulders and neck. Although it felt heavenly, the closeness was beginning to feel oppressive. Gretchen wanted to scream, tear something up, get a sledgehammer and make holes in the wall, cut all her hair off and put on war paint. She didn't feel like calming down.

She was furious with Joanie, Tony, and even more furious with herself for even agreeing to leave the girls alone with such irresponsible people. It was the first time she'd done so for more than an overnight. Never before had she actually left the state or been more than a few hours away by car. She knew better. She feared this could happen, and she'd been right.

It was the last time she'd not trust her intuition, that gut feeling deep down that told her Tony and his new bimbo girlfriend didn't care for the three girls the way she did. The sweet look Clover gave her as she stepped into Joanie's car would haunt her the rest of her life. She shuddered to think it might be the last time she saw her lovely daughter. She leaned forward over her knees, covered her face with her hands, and sobbed.

"Shhh. Shhh, Gretchen. Don't despair yet, sweetie, but I sure know how you feel." Kate was pulling her hair from her neck, rubbing the top of her spine, and trying to soothe her with reassurances.

"The guys will think of something, Gretchen," her sister cooed, but it didn't do any good. "You're not in this alone, sweetheart."

"Just goes to show you big boobs and brains don't go together!" she answered.

Most of the group chuckled. Trace shared a cautious smile with Coop. Kate hugged her from behind. "That's my big sister. I hope you'll have the chance to tell her so and very soon!"

"And I'll be right there to be your second in case you want to take a punch at her," added Linda.

"You'd think Tony would have more of a clue than to leave picking up our daughter to such an airhead. She was probably having her nails done."

"Or getting a spray on tan. She lives in Portland, remember?" answered Linda. "White legs. They don't get out in the sun much."

Kate's stern stare to her sister-in-law stopped her from continuing on with the litany of words it appeared she was going to spew.

Trace knelt at Gretchen's side, kissing her palms and then placing his hands tenderly at the sides of her face. "Baby, Libby is making the arrangements now to get you home. I'm going to go with you to see if I can help out somehow."

"Thank you, Trace, but that's not necessary."

Cooper piped up. "Gretchen, you're not going to let your ex and his girlfriend orchestrate a payoff and the return of Clover. And we have to involve the police."

"No!"

"Honey, you need them," interrupted Trace. "They have training and experience with these things."

"I don't trust them with the life of my daughter." She scanned the group of people assembled around her. "But thank you all. So grateful for your support."

"Not enough, Gretchen," said Kate, her jaw fixed. "You have to let these guys do what they do all the time. They want to come. Let us help you, Gretchen. Think about Clover."

That turned her stomach, and she melted again into a series of sobs. Trace pulled her over towards him, while he slipped onto the couch.

"Let it all out, Gretchen. Believe me, there's no

fuckin' way we're going to let anything happen to Clover. We're going to need a little more information, so we'll coach you for your next call with these guys. But let us help figure out where she is and see if we can get her safely returned. We've already started the process. I promise we'll do everything in our power to bring her back to you."

Gretchen took strength from his steel blue eyes, so steady and unwavering. He wore his conviction on his face. As she looked up at Coop, Fredo, and several of the other SEALs, they bore the same expression.

"Let us help you, Gretchen," Coop asked again. "Libby's found some tickets for a non-stop direct to Portland. Tyler and Ollie and the others will stay behind with the women. But we're your army, little sister. The four of us."

"I'm older than you are, Coop."

"Good. Then it's settled. We're going!" Coop grinned, patting the top of her head.

She barely had time to say anything further before she heard him bark some orders. "Okay, gents, let's get to packing."

Gretchen suddenly realized she hadn't called her parents. "I've got to call mom," she said as she looked at Kate.

"Do it."

Her dad picked the phone up. "Sweetie! Oh God,

Gretchen, it's all over the news. Have you heard from Clover?"

So much for keeping it private.

"How did the news get it?" she asked.

"Tony did an interview at the arena. He begged for them to return his daughter. You know Tony—"

"Well, that's just great because they asked that no one contact the police. Leave it to Tony to screw things up." She squeezed Trace's hand. "Dad, we're coming to Portland, catching a flight out of Lihue at noon. Can I talk to the girls?"

"Your mom took them to the store for a little distraction. They'll be back soon."

"Tell them I'm coming home. And that I love them. Thank God you have them. And give mom a hug."

"Will do, honey. Anything else you want us to do now? Are they asking for money? Have you been able to talk to Clover? She must be scared out of her mind."

"She's holding up. She's a tough kid. And she knows I'm coming. I'm bringing some reinforcements. Some of Tyler's buddies are flying home with me."

"Thank God. That's what we need is a bunch of Navy SEALs right now. Well, you let us know what the plan is, and we'll do whatever. You need money? We'll try to raise some cash."

"No. Don't do anything yet. But if the police contact you, I need a name, okay?"

"You got it, kid. Have a safe flight home. Your mother will be relieved we heard from you."

Kate leaned over Gretchen's shoulder and called out, "Hi, Dad. Love you. We'll see you in a few days."

Gretchen disconnected the call and sat there staring at the empty dial while the beehive of activity happened all around her.

Trace laid her back on the couch—the same one that she'd slept with him all night long, and, just like this morning's early miracle hours, his tender kisses left her gasping for air. She wished she could wake up and find that this had all been a very bad dream.

"Stay here for a minute or two. Just close your eyes, and then we'll get you sorted, and we'll be on our way, okay?" Trace said with a pat to her head.

She nodded. But then the sounds of Clover's terrified voice echoed in her ears, and her eyes filled with tears. Before she could wipe them free, Trace was there, kissing her, rubbing her cheeks with his thumbs, whispering for her not to worry.

He stood. She took one long look at this tall hero with hands the size of basketballs, but with his heart full of passion, showing no fear, only total devotion to the mission at hand. That was when she began to hope that perhaps, if anyone could help her, Trace and his friends could.

SHE FINALLY REACHED Joanie by phone when she arrived at the Lihue airport. The line for security screening was short.

"Oh God, Gretchen, I'm so sorry. Tony and I feel so awful," the bombshell blathered. The more she talked the angrier Gretchen felt.

"Save it. Where the hell is Tony?"

"He's at practice. You know he can't miss practice."

"His daughter has been kidnapped for Christ's sake!"

"Yes, yes, they called us. Tony made a plea on TV for her safe return. The police said it was best to get it out there to the general public."

Gretchen wanted to reach through the phone and strangle her. "Didn't they tell you not to involve the police?"

"I—I don't know. Some reporters were there at the gym interviewing players for the game Sunday night when he got the call. Coach said to take it out on the court, so he made his statement, and then he's going down to the police station. Are you coming home or staying in Hawaii? Tony didn't—"

"Geez, Joanie. What kind of a mother do you think I am? We're at the airport, headed back home." She felt Trace's firm hand on the back of her neck, massaging her, bringing her energy, and letting her feel the closeness and warmth of his body standing like a rock behind her. She saw some of the other passengers look her way and knew from their reaction that Trace had stared them down. She lowered her voice. "How the hell did this happen, Joanie?"

"I had a small accident on the way over to the school. I didn't have Clover's cell phone number. Stupid, I know."

Gretchen realized that Clover probably still had her cell with her. She turned to face Trace and let him know, but was ushered to the Homeland Security Inspector. She put her phone to her shoulder and rummaged for her ticket and her license.

"Turn off your phone, ma'am," the Inspector commanded.

"I've got to go, Joanie. Have Tony call me. I'll be boarding in a little over an hour."

"Yes, yes. No problem. I'll get him to call as soon as I can."

"Cell phone off!" barked another Homeland agent just as she put the phone away. Trace showed his license and ticket and waited for Gretchen to find hers. They made their way through the scanning. Gretchen had to go back a second time because she had left her cell in her pocket.

Finally at the gate, she sat and let out a big sigh. Trace was quick to cover her shoulders with his long arm. His fingers laced along her scalp above her ear, pressing her face to his chest as he continued to rub. The feel of his strength, the steadiness of his hands, and the sound of his deep breathing was all she could think about.

They boarded the plane and soon were off into the big blue skies above the Pacific Ocean, Hawaiian music playing in the background. On any other day, she would have welcomed it, but today, the music sounded mocking and dangerous. The vacation had turned into her greatest nightmare.

"Sleep, Gretchen. That's all you can do right now. Save your strength for when we land, honey. I'm right here." Trace's soothing words helped. He adjusted her seat back to match his, and she fell asleep against his muscled arm, holding his left hand between hers.

CHAPTER 10

As soon as the plane landed, several of the Team's cell phones rang. Gretchen's did as well. Trace noted the number as being the kidnapper when she showed him the dial.

"Let it go to voicemail until we have some privacy," he told her.

Gretchen agreed and turned off the ring. When she checked back, no voicemail had been left.

Her SUV was parked in long-term parking, and the four SEALs loaded the suitcases. Trace took charge of driving with Gretchen riding shotgun up front. Fredo hadn't changed his blue Hawaiian shirt, and Trace chuckled.

"What?" Fredo served him a dose of attitude. "I'm still on vacation, dude. Just not in Hawaii."

"Fredo's right," inserted Coop. "You'll discover soon enough, Gretchen. Hell if I don't actually get excited now that we've got something to do. That beats lying on the beach any day."

Trace considered Coop's comments, and he also began to enjoy the pulse of a Brotherhood op coming up. "Sounds like a vacation to me." But when he glanced at Gretchen, he saw the mistake he'd made. "Sorry," he whispered.

Armando leaned over the seat as Trace exited the parking lot toward the freeway. "Your dad have any guns, Gretchen? Big guns?"

"My parents were hippies, Armando. Sorry, no guns, but I have a .38"

Trace nodded and gave her a wink. "You know how to use it?"

"I took a class and had some practice. Dad insisted."

"He sounds like a good man. Every woman should know how to shoot."

"We'll have to make do with what we've got, then." Armando sighed and sat back into the second seat behind Trace.

"I've got the cell phone data. Registered to a *Casa de Flores*," Coop said as he examined a recent text.

"Never heard of it," said Gretchen.

"My friends can't find an address with that business listing, either."

"Oh, one other thing I forgot to tell you."

Gretchen was holding up well, Trace noted. Her

voice had lowered an octave and was no longer shaking.

"We have a locator on Clover's cell phone. Will that help?" Gretchen frowned.

"You bet. Write her number down," Coop said as he handed her a small spiral notebook.

Then Trace revealed he'd packed a sidearm.

"We all do, Trace," answered Fredo. "I never go anywhere, even on vacation, without some protection."

"Let's hope we don't have to use them. But at least we have something," mumbled Armando.

They arrived at Gretchen's home on a hillside overlooking the panoramic waterway valley. The districts below were covered in row housing and meandering streets, bordering the Columbia River beyond. Rain threatened, and the late afternoon was quickly evaporating.

They parked around the rear of the two-story structure. Gretchen showed them in through the kitchen. With the suitcases brought into the living room, Gretchen got to work making some sandwiches and heating up some soup she had in the pantry.

"Should I attempt to call them back?" she asked as she brought over a plate of fruit.

"Trust me, for a million bucks, they'll call," said Armando.

"I'd try to call. Let them know you're back in

town," offered Trace. "And try your ex again. See what the updates are, if any."

"Good idea," Coop agreed, with his phone to his ear.

"And I'm texting Kate now to let her know we got home safely. She can let my folks know."

When Gretchen tried to redial the number the stranger had called from, it came up with a disconnect. She tried again with the same result.

"He's got a phone that probably blocks incoming calls. Makes the device harder to trace that way," revealed Fredo.

"So let's discuss what we know," said Trace. Gretchen sat next to him, texting her sister.

Coop walked toward the hallway, talking to his contact.

"She's in a warehouse type structure," said Armando.

"It's cold. Probably no heat in the building. We got a business like a wholesale florist, I'm guessing from the name," added Fredo.

"I'm wondering how they knew where she'd be," added Gretchen.

"You think they've been following them? Following the girls?" asked Trace.

"They definitely did some advance work. That might indicate a detailed plan," said Fredo.

"You notice anyone unusual lurking around the house?" Trace questioned her.

She shook her head. "I've been thinking about that. I'm coming up blank. Of course, I was rushing around, getting ready for this trip. I probably wasn't paying attention." She hung her head in shame. Trace squeezed her shoulder.

"Don't blame yourself, Gretchen. Really not your fault," he promised.

"You know, something must have given them the idea. I'm guessing this isn't a big operation, more like the crime of opportunity," Armando added.

"Maybe they thought they'd get Gretchen as well. Perhaps they got lucky when Clover was left all alone? That type of thing, Armando?"

His Team brother shrugged. "Could be. Just speculation. But I'm thinking something planted the thought this would be a good idea."

"You check your messages for anything from the police, Gretchen?" Trace asked her.

She ran to the kitchen and pushed the replay on the answering machine and wrote down the detective's name who left her a message some three hours ago. "I'm going to call him right now."

Before she could do so, her cell rang. She held up the screen, showing the SEALs it was the same number.

"Mrs. Sanders. You are back in Oregon now?"

"Yes." She pushed speakerphone so they could all hear.

"Good. So we have spoken to your husband."

"Ex."

"Ex-husband then. And he has indicated he will be working on raising the necessary cash. I suggest you coordinate with him. But he has violated one of my rules about the police and the press."

"Yes, I just found out about that. We've not been able to talk yet. I've been on the plane coming home."

"This is what he says as well. I am not happy, Mrs. Sanders. Your husband doesn't seem to want to follow the rules. He must be taught a lesson."

Trace tensed, hoping Tony's mistakes were not going to be taken out on Clover.

"So I have raised the bar to $1,500,000 dollars. This is non-negotiable."

Gretchen gasped, but Cooper put his finger to his lips, motioning her to be calm. Trace saw her struggle to stuff down her anger and her growing fear.

"Y-yes. I'm listening."

Good girl, Gretchen, Trace thought.

"He gave permission for you to bring the money to the designated drop-off spot."

Gretchen rolled her eyes. Trace shrugged and motioned for her to continue the dialog.

Cooper held up his notebook, on which he had

written, *ask to speak to Clover again. See if you can get more clues.*

"Okay, we'll work that out," she said to the kidnappers. "But I want to talk to Clover again to make sure she's okay."

"I will give you exactly one minute when I'm done. Tomorrow morning at eleven o'clock, I will call you back, and you will bring the money to the spot I'll designate. You'll only have a few minutes to get there. Are you less than thirty minutes to Clover's school?"

"Yes."

"The drop won't be there, but I will leave further instructions for you at the school."

"H-how will I know?" Gretchen asked.

"It will be explained tomorrow. Now, would you like to speak with Clover?"

"Yes, please."

They all heard the teen's fragile voice start in with the same refrain she'd had earlier. "Mom, when are you coming to get me?"

"Soon, baby." She looked at Coop for further instructions since he was writing furiously in his notebook. Gretchen read it over quickly and then repeated the instructions he'd written. "Did they take you far, sweetheart? Was it—?"

The sound of the phone dropping gave Trace the chills.

"Mrs. Sanders, you were told not to make tricks with me. I am going to be very angry if you don't behave. It's going to be a long evening. You don't want me anywhere near your daughter when I get angry."

"I'm sorry. I just—"

"Your full compliance is required, Mrs. Sanders."

The last sentence was drowned out by the sounds of a locomotive blast in the background and then what appeared to be a rumbling echo as the train was accelerating. The men stiffened and took notice.

"No more tricks. Tomorrow at eleven then."

"Sir, please, may I—?"

But the phone had already gone dead.

"We need a Portland map of the rail lines. You have something like that here, Gretchen?" asked Coop.

"I can get it online." She pulled out her laptop from her carry-on bag and began the internet search. Finding the page she wanted, she turned the computer to face Coop and Trace, who studied it side-by-side.

"Wish Tyler was here. He grew up in Portland," muttered Gretchen.

"I think we have what we need," said Trace. "Look. There's a station house, and it's a hub. We've got what appears to be about four sets of tracks all parallel there. The only other one I see is downtown Portland." Trace stood up. "Wouldn't we have heard cars and other city activity?"

"Good thinking. So, Gretchen, what is this area here called?" asked Coop.

"We just call it the warehouse waterfront district. Used to be the cheapest loft rentals in the city, but now it's gotten trendy. Still, many of those buildings are abandoned," she answered.

"Is it close to the school?" Trace asked.

"Very close. Yes."

Coop's phone rang. After a brief discussion, he ended his call with a "Thanks, buddy. I owe you one again." He smiled to his audience. "Okay, he gave me coordinates that said between the river and Brickyard. North is the Pallatine Bridge, and south is the entrance to the 305 freeway. He said that was about a ten block radius."

"Brickyard is right here." Gretchen pointed out the labeled street. "And the rails run right through the first third of that square you just gave me. All the new upscale lofts are along the river, so I'd guess they'd be somewhere around here."

Trace was starting to feel hopeful. "Good job, sweetheart. You know that area at all?"

"Lots of homeless shelters. Some rescue missions and a couple brew pub houses. The whole place is undergoing massive renovation so there are construction projects all over. Closed streets. It's a mess getting through there."

"But we didn't hear any construction, either. Just the trains," said Trace.

"I don't ever go there alone. Sometimes, the church youth group would help out serving Thanksgiving Dinner down there, but as a big group. Not a place to go to at night by yourself."

"And that's why you're not going by yourself," he told her.

"Good deal. I can live with that," said Coop. "How many buildings are in that area?"

Gretchen sat down again and put her palm to her forehead. "Tons."

"Explain what you mean by tons," said Fredo.

She stared at her hands neatly folded on the tabletop. "I'm going to guess and say more than fifty. At least."

CHAPTER 11

TONY SANDERS CALLED her about the same time as the police showed up at her door. She put the call on speaker so everyone could hear their conversation.

"Holy crap, Tony. What were you thinking—going on TV!"

"Wait a minute before you go all commando on me. I was following orders from our General Manager. He's dealt with things like this before. He said TV was a great tool."

"God, Tony, Clover is *your* daughter, not theirs. They just care about ratings. Of course, TV is their friend. Are you that stupid?" Gretchen had worked herself up and was not going to back down to him now.

"I'm doing the best I can. So lay off me, Gretchen."

"How could you let Joanie—"

"Joanie is real sorry about all this."

Gretchen's stomach churned at Tony's Bimbo Defense.

"I'm beyond that, Tony. They say they want the money tomorrow. And they've upped their price to a million five, thanks to your good judgment following the instructions from your 'handlers.' Are they going to provide the cash, too?"

She was surprised at her control. The last thing she wanted to do was show Tony how scared and helpless she felt, even with the SEALs at her side.

The police were questioning the men on Trace's team, but looking in her direction. She interrupted her ex's response. "Tony, the police are here."

"They'll accompany you and give you a vest to wear."

"A *vest*? You volunteered to send me out there with a vest?" She felt her blood pressure rise again. "Did it ever occur to you I might be the next victim here?"

"Don't get all crazy on me, Gretchen. What the hell was I supposed to do? Not like he gave me much choice."

"Nice of you to offer me up. You coward. What happened to your balls, Tony? You sure got 'em when you go clubbing, especially when there's a blonde you haven't banged within a ten block radius."

"That's not fair. Look, the team's got insurance. I *can't* deliver the cash. And yes, they're paying most of it on a loan to me."

"Oh, that's right. They own you. The team before family, right? Well, if Joanie had been on time, none of this would have happened!"

"Oh yeah? Well, perhaps she would have been taken hostage as well. Did you for once ever think about anyone but yourself?"

Gretchen was livid. "You complete asshole. You are a worthless human being. A worthless husband and less than worthless father. You don't even deserve to have the company of those three beautiful girls, and if I have my way, you'll be not spending any time with them soon."

She knew it was wrong, but the pressure of the events had set her off. His lazy attitude added fuel to the fire.

"Okay, big shot. I'm going to bring you one-point-five million dollars in cash tomorrow after the banks open. Let's see how well you do suing me for custody. I think you're a reckless mother to go off on an island vacation, screwing who knows how many guys, leaving your daughters behind. Angela is only four!"

"And she doesn't like spending any time with you already. And I was with Kate and Tyler and their friends."

"At an orgy house, I hear."

She was going to object, but she saw Trace and a detective walk toward her. She'd gone way over the top and now had dug herself a big hole.

"I'm not sure where you get your facts, Tony, but as usual, you're completely wrong."

"Check the morning paper, Gretchen. *Mother of kidnapped daughter on romantic Tropical Tryst in Hawaii.*"

Her face turned bright red.

The detective extended his hand. "I'm gonna have to jump in here. Let me talk to him."

Gretchen agreed. Trace kept his distance, which was a good thing. Right now, she didn't want anyone's hug. She was looking for the sledgehammer in her fantasy life.

The detective turned off the speaker, introduced himself, and then gave Tony a sage piece of advice. "Son, luckily, I don't have to do a lot of these types of things on a daily basis, but I'll tell you what. It makes no sense to accuse and abuse those around you who are only trying to help. I think you need to keep your mouth shut, and that goes for any more television interviews."

The detective listened to Tony give some explanation.

"Yeah, well, you let the coach do his job with the Trailblazers and their organization. We're trying to save your daughter's life, and that's a whole other thing. Now, if they contact you again, you let me know.

You have my card."

He listened to Tony again, shaking his head and rolling his eyes. Gretchen liked the detective immediately.

"Well, that's fine son, but these leaks to the paper are not going to do your girls any good when they go back to school. Just think about it. For their sake, keep your fuckin' mouth *shut*."

Without allowing Tony to give more excuses, the detective hung up the phone and handed it back to Gretchen. He warily looked at the four SEALs standing in front of him.

"I've got a hunch none of you is going to get much sleep tonight. We'll patrol the warehouse area where you think they are holding her, but we don't do anything until tomorrow morning. Understood?"

Gretchen knew the SEALs were lying when they shook their heads yes. He addressed Gretchen. "You need to get some sleep, Mother. Tomorrow is going to be a very big day. I'll post a guard, and we'll patrol your neighborhood. We'll be in touch if we get any breaking developments, and I'll tell you the same thing I told him. Focus on your daughter. Try to think about how she's feeling tonight, all alone, stuck with a bunch of strangers. Let's not do anything to jeopardize our success tomorrow."

"Thank you, Detective," Gretchen whispered.

He started for the door and then stopped. "I have to say this one more thing, sweetheart. Everyone in town knows who your husband is. You can tell him after the fact that he's the reason they went after her. He's the goose that laid the golden egg. So let him do his job and you don't speak to him anymore unless you got one of your boyfriends here to chaperone. Am I getting through?"

"They're not my boyfriends." She saw Trace bite his lip. "Only one is. But that's sage advice, Detective. Thanks for your time. I'll let you know if they make further contact."

She accepted his card and then shook his hand, and again, he headed for the doorway. He gave the SEALs a long conspiratorial look.

Gretchen suspected he understood just what they were going to do tonight. Tomorrow was indeed going to be a very big day.

CHAPTER 12

TRACE KNEW THE lack of specialized equipment severely handicapped them. But their experience and training was far superior to anything else on the planet, and in that, he had complete confidence. They hadn't had the time to rehearse over and over again, sometimes re-creating their mission over a hundred times before they set out. But they had intuition. It wouldn't be the first time they were in an unfamiliar town, going after people they'd never seen or met before. But without firepower, specialty explosive charges Fredo was legendary for creating, it was like doing an op blindfolded.

Their odds were still better than most.

Then there was the raw truth that all four of the SEALs were pumped up and ready to go, without having a moment's hesitation to risk their lives to save Clover. And maybe it was a good thing all they had were their sidearms. They were not supposed to interfere with local law enforcement. They were officially supposed to defer to them. They weren't even allowed to use their guns except in cases of self-defense, and then only on rare occasions.

But there was no doubt about it. This was a snatch and grab mission, without their gear. He hoped the bad guys were not well trained or armed. Then the odds would be hugely in the SEALs' favor.

The evening had come full upon them, and as they made their way down to the warehouse district, he noted the stars looks lackluster compared to the bright twinkling orbs in Hawaii. He vowed to take Gretchen and her daughters back there, if he were given the chance. He hoped he could make that happen.

He also hoped he was given the opportunity to meet Gretchen's ex, and give him a lecture to let him know what a douchbag he thought the man was. But all that could be accomplished after they had succeeded. And if they didn't, all bets were off.

Coop directed him where to drive. Gretchen had insisted on coming with them and talked over his shoulder, pointing out places she knew.

Coop angled his face and cleared his throat. "I'm going to ask you to call your daughter's cell phone. They might not have turned it off, since we got a good triangulation out of the signal. But they could destroy the phone if they get wind of what we're trying to do."

"Wouldn't my location finder help?" She'd brought her laptop. "Can't I just look it up on here?"

"You can ask the phone company to ping it," said Armando.

"We don't have the equipment to pick it up. But sure, go ahead and try."

Gretchen directed Trace to stop in front of one of the missions, thinking they might have internet.

"Nope. No signal. Any one of you have a hotspot?"

None of the SEALs did.

She directed him to drive in front of a coffee house down the street where she was able to log into their WIFI, which was strong enough to use while she was seated in the car. The red dot located an intersection, but then moved around and targeted another intersection. Then another. Trace tried to head in the general direction of the signal, but at last stopped.

"They put this on a dog or something?" Fredo asked.

"I think that's exactly what they did. Or in someone's backpack. Damn. This isn't going to help," Cooper muttered.

They watched as the red locator moved briefly outside the box that had been created with the triangulation. And then it strangely moved back inside.

"I think we should follow it. Check it out," said Trace.

Coop shrugged. “Everyone keep an eye out for Casa de Flora. They may not know we have that name.”

The streets were in shadow. Half the lights had been broken. Pieces of broken glass littered the sidewalks and shone in the moonlight like diamonds. Flocks of ashen-colored people in baggy clothes huddled over trash barrels set ablaze to keep them warm. They passed several rescue missions, most of them with lines going down the street.

Gretchen offered an explanation as Trace turned the corner, the headlights scanning the shabby crowd. “They take only a certain number each night. Most of them sleep in the meeting rooms or the sanctuary, on cots or the church pews. And these are the lucky ones.”

“It’s a shame. Reminds me of our project in San Diego, right, Fredo? But this looks worse. No families,” said Armando.

“Oh, they’re here, but they wouldn’t dare go outside now,” answered Gretchen. “This is a very dangerous area, constantly involved in turf wars. Clover might have even been here a time or two with her youth group. But not at night. Never at night.”

“She’s a good kid, Gretchen. I think you’ve done well.” Armando smiled. Trace watched in the rear view mirror as Gretchen couldn’t help but blush at his good looks, even in the evening shadows.

Trace aimed toward the red dot again, which had temporarily stopped in one place. Coming into view were the bright lights of a liquor store, so they waited outside with the car running. Some teens smoked cigarettes just outside the door when a young, lanky youth exited the store and joined them.

"That's Clover's backpack!" exclaimed Gretchen.

Trace focused on the newcomer. As the group ambled down the street, under the light of a streetlamp he could see that the backpack was black and red with the distinctive hurricane logo of the Portland Trailblazers. Dangling from one of the zipper pockets was a small pink teddy bear.

"You stay here, Gretchen, and keep the doors locked," Trace said as he shut the motor down, and they moved away from the SUV in pairs.

Fredo and Armando came at the group from the right rear, and Trace and Cooper walked straight toward the boys. About ten feet before confrontation, Cooper spoke up.

"You guys know where I can score a little weed, man?"

As one of the taller boys delved into his own black backpack, Trace saw Armando and Fredo rip Clover's backpack from the kid, sending him on his knees. The crowd turned and were greeted with a couple of SigSauers.

"We want no trouble. Just want the backpack and your friend here," Armando said. He walked up to the youth, yanked on his shirt collar, and stood him up on his feet. The group was about to chance a fight when they were stopped by Cooper and Trace, also showing firearms. The kids disappeared into the streets, scattering all over the place.

They dragged their prey back to the SUV and slammed him up against it. Armando checked his pockets carefully and spilled his contents of pills, bags of powder, and some loose weed all over the street. The kid swore but was given a swift kick to his butt.

Trace examined the contents of the backpack and, in addition to more drugs, found a book, a binder, some loose papers, a zipper bag of pencils, some deodorant, and a chap stick, as well as a change of girl's underwear. He also found a half-eaten energy bar. Crusty with sticky flakes from the opened bar, Trace found Clover's cell phone at the very bottom and turned it back on.

"So where did you get this?" Fredo asked the kid, holding up the backpack.

"In a dumpster."

"Show me." Fredo pushed him toward the street.

The youth started to run, but Cooper easily caught up and tackled him, sending his face to the pavement.

"You wanna play hide and seek? I like playing that

game, except you're gonna get all messed up. And oh wow. Look at that. You've got a bloody nose."

The boy cursed.

"So you gonna show us this time?" Fredo repeated.

Armando stood him up again by hoisting his collar, and the boy scanned the faces of the four SEALs. At last, he nodded.

They asked Gretchen to move to the third seat, while Armando and Fredo babysat the boy in the second seat. He turned around briefly, taking note of Gretchen. Then he pointed, and Trace followed directions.

"So you meet the people who left this behind, son?" Coop asked him.

He shook his head.

"Did you see the people who dumped this backpack?"

Again, he shook his head.

They stopped at a large green dumpster outside a brick two-story warehouse building. Armando held the boy while Fredo jumped into the dumpster and then began to sneeze. "Dammit. Flowers in here. I'm fuckin' going to be sneezing all night with my allergies," he grumbled. He sneezed several more times and swore in between in Spanish.

Coop chuckled. "I think he can go," he said to Armando, still clutching the boy by his collar. The Puerto

Rican SEAL shoved the kid, and he ran into the night.

Trace scrambled to the front of the building and saw the letters on a glass door. "Casa de Flora." Inside, it looked like a clean little flower shop with refrigerators containing bunches of bouquets of flowers in white metal cones. He went back and reported to the others.

Armando returned from the other side, breathing heavily. "There's a roll-up door to the warehouse on the other side and another side door about ten feet in front. No door on the rear. The roll-up isn't padlocked, but the side door is locked."

"Fredo, can you pick the front door lock first?" asked Coop.

"No tools, Coop. But wait a minute!" He hopped back into the dumpster and the sneezing began. He climbed out clutching a bundle of discarded florist's wire. "I can use this, I think. Be right back."

"Trace, you go let Gretchen know what's happening. Tell her to stay inside the SUV again, but keep her head down."

As Coop discussed several of their options, Trace tapped on the window, and Gretchen leaned over the rear seat, opening the driver side rear door. "We're about to breach the building. You stay put and keep it locked. The keys are still in the ignition, okay?"

"Do we know it's them?"

"I think so, sweetheart. The name of the flower shop matches the cell phone record Coop got from his friend at NSA. So we're treating this as a go. We'll split up. Anything goes wrong, you call 9-1-1 immediately, okay?"

"What about the detective?"

"Call him second. 9-1-1 gets the paramedics and a shitpile of others."

She took in a deep breath. "Trace, thank you so much. I—"

His name was being whispered, so he had to cut her off with a swift kiss, pointed to the lock, and joined Armando at the roll-up. Coop headed up front to meet Fredo, who had already entered the flower shop. Their watches had been set, and on the mark, Trace pulled back the latch as Armando threw his full weight into raising the metal accordion material. Trace immediately grabbed the other side, and together, they got the door fully raised in less than thirty seconds.

Prepared for firepower, they each rolled into the shadows, Armando on the right and Trace on the left. They heard the rattle of a semi-automatic of low caliber, sounding more like a child's toy. Trace fell into some water and realized he'd encountered a shallow tray holding dozens of pot plants, each covered with large sacks of burlap. The distinctive skunky smell of growing marijuana made his nose itch.

Fredo and Coop joined him, but before could warn his buddy, Fredo erupted into a spasm of uncontrollable sneezes that nearly sent him to the ground. They could still hear voices on the other side of a partition built that spanned the two brick outer walls.

"Anyone have a match?" Armando whispered.

Between his convulsions, Fredo managed to find a set of waterproof matches in a pocket and handed them over.

"This fertilizer is highly flammable." He'd removed the fist-sized rubber lid. "We gotta roll this closer."

Trace helped him tip the barrel on its side, centering it on the door. Liquid fertilizer leaked all over the room.

"Try not to get that on your clothes or you'll catch fire, Trace. If you have to, dive into the trays."

"Wait, what about Clover?" he asked, pointing to the doorway.

"She'd be against a wall, not a doorway. This gives us a way in."

"Gotcha."

"Take cover on the count of three. The explosion might take down part of the roof, too, so watch your head." Armando didn't wait for Trace's acknowledgement. He struck the match and tossed it into the open mouth of the now leaking barrel, and they both ran to opposite sides of the building as fast as they could.

The explosion did indeed take out the doorway. In fact, there was nothing left of it. The blast had extended to the ceiling and ignited the cross bracing on the domed roof. They could hear screaming inside the space, as well as broken glass shattering all around them.

All four of the SEALs ran through the flames. Trace was glad his clothes had gotten soaked. They spread out. Several times, Trace stepped over bodies, examining them carefully, hoping not to find Clover among them. He heard sounds of a struggle here and there as other members of his team immobilized several of the surprised and severely injured kidnappers. But the more seconds ticked by, the more worried he got. His eyes were stinging, and he recognized the signs he'd inhaled too much of the toxic smoke.

Finally, he heard something that made his day.

"I said get your hands off me, you cretin!" The voice was crackly just like a fourteen-year-old's. A very pissed off fourteen-year-old.

Clover had evidently delivered a blow to someone who had tried to handle her, and she'd managed to send him crashing to the ground with a groan.

"Mom? Mom, are you there?"

Trace slammed into her. He wrapped his arms around her, though she struggled. She kneed his groin and tried to pick out his eyes with her fingers. He was so busy trying to drag her to safety, his throat so raw, that when he tried to tell her to stop, all that came out was a rasping squeak.

"Clover," he finally managed to eek out.

But she continued to struggle. By the time he got her outside the roll up door and into fresh air, he was ready to pass out. Yet he held on as he fell to the ground and wouldn't let go.

Blackness crept into his vision. The sounds of the crackling fire subsided. Everything started looking like it was in slow motion. Echoes of his past, sounds of the waves on the beach, muffled screams of friends he'd lost in battle filled his ears.

So this is how it goes, then. You do see your past.

Someone's hand slapped the side of his face, but he still wouldn't let go. The numbness was welcome. He was out of pain. The screaming continued, but it sounded comical, and he started to chuckle.

"I'm not letting you go, Clover. I promised. I promised."

And then everything went to black.

CHAPTER 13

GRETCHEN WAITED IN the emergency room lobby for word on Trace. Clover had been treated for minor cuts and bruises and some smoke inhalation. She'd broken two bones in her hand trying to get away from Trace's relentless grip when she mistook him for one of the bad guys. But when the results of her chest x-ray came in, she was deemed well enough to be discharged at the end of the day after what was left of a night's sleep.

Clover's fingers were immobilized, and she finally got a shower and a change of clothes she'd desperately wanted. Clean, warm, and near the ones she loved, Clover's pink cheeks returned, and she began to express worry about her mother. Gretchen shrugged it off and tried not to let her concern for Trace show. There was time enough to have the "talk" with Clover, if and when that time was right. Tonight was about getting rest and healing.

Gretchen had spent nearly an hour with her before she finally retired, holding her, helping her to call her sisters and her grandparents.

So when Trace was moved to a room, they allowed her to accompany him. She was exhausted, but was much more comfortable waiting for news in a hospital bed next to him than in the waiting room filled with too many voices and activity. There were not enough beds in the ICU, which is where he belonged, the doctor told her, but he'd be treated the same, just without some of the equipment.

Trace had been taken to the hospital unconscious, and when they last checked, he was still unconscious. The specialists were worried about his lungs. Although a portable chest x-ray didn't reveal anything serious, problems were likely to develop later on.

His brothers had also been treated, and although it was recommended they stay in the hospital overnight, they weren't having any of it. They sat with Gretchen and continued the vigil right with her every step of the way.

As the early morning hours turned into dawn, Gretchen awoke to the sounds of heavy snoring. Fredo had tried to sleep in the lounge chair usually reserved for nursing moms or senior citizens. His knees were pulled to his chest as he curled up around a pillow at his side.

Coop's ankles and nearly half of his lower legs hung off the couch, which had been moved from the vacant waiting room. He was on his back, and Gretchen had asked for and received a blanket to cover his chest up. Both his hands had been burned and, due to their size, resembled white boxing gloves after the treatment.

Armando slept with his chest and arms draped over Trace's bed, his head buried in the blanket to ward off the oncoming sunrise. He was seated in a chair, his upper torso bent at the waist.

Gretchen had slept in the bed in Patient Number Two's slot, which finally had been offered after all the evening shift nurses were unsuccessful peeling the SEALs off the floor in order to give her a seat. They gave her a hospital gown to wear, a towel and soap for a shower in the morning. She was grateful for the courtesy.

Trace had ointment on his eyes and a breathing mask, along with an IV in his right arm. He hadn't moved since they'd brought him. His clothes had been cut off, the pieces of the sooty fabric in a large blue hospital bag, hanging from the chair Armando was sitting in.

As she studied him, his quiet repose belied how sick he really was. The vision of his chest gently rising and falling with each breath got blurry when tears welled up and spilled over her cheeks. It wasn't lost on her the story that Clover revealed, how Trace hung on to her no matter how hard she hit him. Her teen felt awful about it, but at the same time, Gretchen knew he wouldn't abandon her no matter if it cost him his life. It made a huge impression on her oldest. Even if Trace would not go on to become a permanent fixture in their lives, that life lesson he bestowed on her daughter was worth the entire world in gold.

She'd be eternally grateful.

So she'd come to this juncture in her life, along a rocky pathway filled with disappointments while every day living her life for her girls. Now she found she had someone else so precious it was unimaginable that he would not be there in the coming days and months. She knew it was selfish to expect much and way too soon to even say she had a relationship with this man. But something about him told her he was tough, just like she was. A survivor of the love wars. Someone, like herself, who had been unloved and probably mistreated. Whatever was in store for the two of them, she knew it would be worth it in the long run.

Instead of dwelling on any kind of future, she found herself just asking for his healing, to be restored to his particular brand of perfection with that quirky smile and the dark stubble on his cheeks and chin contrasting with his deep blue eyes. Once he was healthy, he'd be in a position to make some decisions, and she would not obligate him nor beg. It had to be something of his own choosing. She just prayed he be given the chance to make that choice, whatever it was.

She wiped her eyes with the sheet again. When she looked back over at him, he'd turned, opened his eyes, and stared right back at her. She wondered if he'd suffered brain injury; he had no expression and didn't try to talk or move a muscle.

He tried to say something, but creases formed at the top of his nose as his raspiness appeared to hurt him. But it didn't stop him. He tried again, and again, all he could get was a small squeak, which was enough to awaken Armando.

"Holy fuck, you didn't die after all."

She could see Trace trying not to laugh. He wasn't looking at Armando, but remained staring back at her. Cooper and Fredo were at the bedside, too, asking him questions. Coop was even checking his pulse, raising his eyelids, and listening to his chest with a stethoscope left over the bedrail. But Trace didn't take his eyes off Gretchen.

"You did good, you big dufus. Now if you irritate me, I'll just punch you, and it will be like a marshmallow punch," Coop said, air-punching close to his face.

Gretchen watched a tear streak down into his pillow. Once more he tried to say something, and this time, she understood him.

"Clover?" he was asking.

Gretchen leaned on her side and gave him a big smile. "She's going to be fine. She's sleeping right now, which is what you should be doing."

"Yes, ma'am," he whispered.

Coop, Fredo, and Armando got the full import of the fact that Trace wasn't in the least bit interested in them. He didn't look at Coop's boxing gloves. Fredo showed him the burn on his right forearm and another angry scrape to his side. Armando had a bandage over his forehead from a glass cut during the explosion and several other bandages on his arms. But Trace didn't react.

Finally, Fredo had had enough. He jumped up and landed on Trace's bed, causing him to bounce to near sitting position. That got his attention.

"*Amigo*. Join the living."

"I am. I'm right here with you all. It's just that"—he turned his face again to stare back at her—"I've just found the most beautiful view in the whole world, and it's a shame she can't see it."

Gretchen touched her chest with her palm and allowed her tears to flow.

"Come here," Trace said. He kneed Fredo off the bed, flipped up his sheets and covers, and showed her his bare legs underneath, scooting to the side to make room for her. He did all this sporting a huge boner.

"You are a mean motherfucker, Trace Bennett," Fredo announced in mock offense.

"Yea but I sound like a pussy cat," Trace whispered in return. All four of the SEALs laughed together. As the silence returned, Trace added one other request. "Help her get over here so I can feel her naked beside me. That's the best kind of medicine right now. And then get the fuck out of my room for, oh, say about three days, okay?"

They took turns messing with him and then dutifully brought her over to his bedside. "Take that stupid hospital gown off her and close your eyes, dammit," he continued to whisper.

Gretchen was beginning to giggle uncontrollably as one of them untied the gown and someone else pulled it away from her body, and she stood in front of Trace completely naked.

"Now that's more like it," he whispered. "Gretchen, get your butt in here, and give me your medicine."

CHAPTER 14

THE PORTLAND TELEVISION stations made the foiled kidnapping attempt huge news. The story had all the earmarks of a blockbuster, even making it to the networks. Tony was a much-beloved star with the Trailblazers, partly because of his antics as a bad boy. The fact that four Navy SEALs rescued his daughter made the story grow to gargantuan proportions. And then there was the drug ring angle, the ransom demand—which was exaggerated to over two million dollars, all the interviews Tony was doing, and the fact that no one lost their lives in the process.

Gretchen put her foot down about Clover doing any interviews, but TV crews camped outside her door the day the story broke. They even followed her to the grocery market and, despite a City ordinance, to the girls' schools.

Trace and the other SEALs were given an award by the mayor, who was also a big Trailblazers fan and responsible for keeping the team in Portland. It all worked well. No guns were used, or so the story went, but large caches of weapons and drugs were seized.

It turned out that one of the janitors at Clover's school had heard Tony give a pep talk to the girls volleyball team. He and his brothers had been in and out of trouble all during their youths. He saw this as their opportunity to score big.

He used to watch Clover being picked up by her mom day after day when practice was over. The brothers hatched a plan, never intending to hurt her, but knew the Trailblazers would cough up the money.

AFTER TRACE GOT out of the hospital two days later, he wanted to spend more alone time with Gretchen, but time was not on their side. His days were growing short. He put in for an extra week for medical purposes, but he knew he couldn't push that more than he had. Already a "Bone Frog" or silver-haired SEAL, and new to Kyle's squad, it meant he still needed to prove himself.

His first mission with the Team was coming up. If he missed that, his longevity as a SEAL would be compromised. Another young froglette would replace him—someone without the wear and tear of hundreds of HALO jumps and strenuous PT workouts. He needed to do something other than blow up a warehouse with one of Fredo's matches.

He declined all the interviews, but couldn't get out of the award ceremony with the mayor. The other three Teammates took off right after, and he planned to follow in six more days. Six very short days. Not much time at all.

His mission was to convince Gretchen to move down to San Diego, where he could eventually get her to move in with him, if everything worked out. But the girls had school and roots in the Portland community. He and Gretchen barely had time to discuss anything. It was going to be tough.

When he came home from the hospital, he slept in Clover's room, alone. This was Gretchen's request. He understood he was going to have to rely on her to introduce him properly to the daughters and their daily routine, or he'd have no chance at all with her.

So the next six days were critical. Though he barely knew her, he knew that this would be the most important mission of his life. If he blew it, he decided he'd go down to the Scupper and join Morgan Hansen's Bone Frog Brotherhood—the group started for the single guys who kept striking out with women. At least he could be part of that family. The beer would help. The ladies who frequented the SEAL bars were never a problem for him. But he was after the brass ring, not the party central crowd. He wanted that one special lady he could love, honor, and protect for the rest of his life. He thought there was more than a little chance Gretchen could be the one.

Clover opened the door to her bedroom and shouted, "Breakfast." Then she slammed it shut behind her. She was as tough as any instructor he'd had in BUD/S. But he'd caught her glancing his way more than once. He was just going to give her time and not force any friendship. It was thin ice. So much of this was out of his control. But it was the only way it could happen.

Having been summarily ordered to the breakfast table, he hoisted himself out of the pink sheets and way too soft mattress, slipped his jeans over his boxers, smelled the pits of a tee shirt he'd worn yesterday and deemed it acceptable enough, brushed his hair and his teeth, gave himself a "It's showtime!" smile in the mirror, and headed downstairs in his bare feet.

Gretchen was dressed. He went weak at the knees recalling the steamy night they'd had, how they kept holding their hands over each other's mouths all the while they were fucking, trying desperately not to wake the girls. The way little Rebecca stared down at her plate without making eye contact with him told Trace they'd not been quiet enough.

Yes, it's a lot to take in. I'm trespassing on your father's territory. Except that jerk doesn't deserve you.

But he knew full well, no matter how bad Tony's

behavior was, their loyalties would always side with him, and there wasn't anything Trace could do about it.

Gretchen blushed and slid herself next to Trace, allowing his right upper arm to feel the space between her breasts very discretely. She smelled wonderful, and her wry smile told him she was enjoying herself.

Tease me all you want, sweetheart. I'll get even tonight. Or maybe this afternoon if you finish all the dropping off and picking ups.

He gave that look to her long enough so she'd share eye contact. "You smell great, and you're the most beautiful cook I've ever met."

Clover had her ear nestled in the open palm of her hand, her elbow on the table, slouching, eating a bowl of cereal. But this made her sit up and roll her eyes when Rebecca and Angie looked to her for a reaction.

Yeah, so I'm gonna make lots of mistakes. I'm patient. Give me a chance, girls.

Like Gretchen had read his thoughts, she gave a soft command, "Clover, sit up straight and eat like a lady."

And all three of the girls sat up, focusing back on their breakfast, and ignored him.

Several minutes of silence was followed by the sound of a car horn honking.

"April's here," announced Rebecca. "Mom, can I

have the two dollars for chocolate milk this week?"

"Sure. Let me go upstairs and get my purse, and then—"

"I got it," Trace said, forgetting himself. He pulled out two crumpled dollar bills from his jeans pocket and laid them on the table in front of Rebecca. The three girls examined the paper money unfolding like it was the last throes of a dying rat, and then they all gave him the look as if he was some sort of alien being.

Which of course he was.

He was on his own. Gretchen didn't come to his defense, which was good. "It's only two dollars, and I wanted to save your mother a trip upstairs, that's all. No big deal, ladies." He went back to his eggs and pretended to ignore them. He hoped to God it was the right move. Women were complicated. Girls were women becoming complicated without any of the coping tools.

And like baby rattlesnakes, they were deadly.

Clover and Rebecca slipped on their coats and backpacks by the rear door off the kitchen. Trace's two dollars was still making a stain on the breakfast table. Gretchen reached over, picked them up, and handed them to her middle daughter.

"Here you go, and say thank you to Mr. Bennett."

Trace looked up to see her fire off her 'thank you' without a smile. Gretchen hugged and kissed them both, reminded the two of what their afternoon schedule was, then walked them through the back porch and out onto the driveway to see that they got into the carpool mom's car. He heard her exchanging words with April, but was just far enough away not to make out any of the specific words.

Angela slipped out of her chair and took up Rebecca's seat next to Trace, scooting it first a little closer to him. He felt he was going to get a lecture from this precocious four-year-old.

"That wasn't very nice of Rebecca and Clover. They should have said good-bye." Angie's honest blue eyes reflected a self-confidence he seldom noticed in a child so young.

"That's a very nice thing for you to say, Angie. Thank you for that."

"No problem. I have good manners. It's important."

With that settled, Trace was feeling encouraged that at least he'd managed to soften one heart of the three.

Angela folded her hands neatly on the table, which came chest-high on her little body.

Here it comes.

"Do you like dogs, Mr. Bennett?"

"Yes, I do. Very much."

"Mom says we can get a dog, a big dog that barks."

She wrinkled her face to show her canines.

"A dog for protection," added Trace, nodding his approval.

"Yes. Because after you go home, it will just be us all alone again."

Trace's breath hitched on the matter-of-fact way Angie said *after you go home.* Had Gretchen told them he was merely here as a thank you for the rescue and then he'd be gone? Of course, it made perfect sense, but he was surprised she'd done that.

"Do you like the beach, Angie?"

"Yes. But in the summer. Too cold right now."

"I know some beaches that are warm all the time. That's where I live. Maybe some time you could come down and I can show them to you. Would you like that?"

Angie nodded. A second later, she hit him with a question he didn't know how to answer. "Are you and mommy getting naked all the time now?"

He tilted his head to see if Gretchen was on her way back to save him, but when she didn't appear, he decided to take a chance. "Well, not all the time. But I get the feeling you all know that your mommy and I like each other."

"How much do you have to like each other to get naked?"

Hoping Gretchen would enter the kitchen any second, he stumbled along with this very tough interview. "Well, I think you should like each other a lot before you get naked. I mean, you reserve that spot for someone very special in your life."

"Did you know I have a daddy?"

"Oh, yes. I haven't met him, though."

"My daddy plays basketball. It's his job. He does some bad things sometimes. He makes Mommy cry a lot."

"That should never be. Your mommy is a wonderful lady, and I happen to know she'd do anything for you."

"Yes. I think she's happy now."

"Really? And what makes you say that?"

"Because she smiles more. I think she's pretty when she smiles, don't you?"

Trace gently put his arm around the little girl's shoulders and whispered, "I happen to completely agree with you, Angie. Your mommy is *spectacular*, especially when she smiles."

Her lips formed a straight flat line, but her eyes smiled and then let a big grin take over her face, revealing two upper teeth missing. Trace removed his arm so as not to scare her and watched Angela sit back with a satisfied look on her face, her arms crossed.

Gretchen entered through the back door and noticed Angela had changed seats. She pretended not to notice. "Want another cup of coffee, Trace?"

"Yes, ma'am. Love some. Do you have time to join me?"

She brought the pot over and filled up his cup. "I'm afraid not," she said as she returned the carafe and started rinsing dishes. "I have to get Angie off to preschool. She has to be there in an hour, and it's clear across town."

"You want some company, then?"

She beamed. "Angie, what do you think? Want to show Mr. Bennett your classroom and introduce him to some of your friends?"

"I think that would be cool," Angie answered. "But, Mommy, who do I say he is? I can't tell them he's the one who gets naked with you, can I?"

CHAPTER 15

GRETCHEN TOOK TRACE to one place he'd never expect. It was to be the first of two tests she wanted to try out on him. He'd insisted on driving after Angie was dropped off, so she directed him to the parking lot of the International Rose Test Garden. The garden was just beginning to bloom out, and the buds were still moist from a light misting of rain that would be going on and off all day. The walkways and paths also had a spectacular view of the city and the river basin beyond.

"Roses. So you like roses, I take it," Trace said as he helped her out of the car, but kept holding her hand, tucking it inside the right pocket of the Navy Pea Coat that had belonged to her ex. Trace had come from Hawaii without any intention of stopping anywhere wet and cold, so he would have frozen to death without it. She was surprised that it fit perfectly on his muscular frame. Tony was probably taller than Trace, but he didn't have the huge shoulders of this handsome SEAL.

"I have about twenty rose bushes of my own back at the house. I love watching how they tend for them here. I don't quite have the green thumb these guys have, but every year, I find something new. Occasionally, I can actually find them at the nursery."

They walked along the crushed granite path between rows of deep green and red-brown new leaves of the compact bushes. Their tops and sides held spikes of velvet color bursts, some of them variegated or tipped in white looking like they'd been dipped in white chocolate. The aroma was heavenly.

"So tell me your favorite," he requested.

This tickled her, and she stared down at her feet, feeling the casual comfort of their gait together in tandem. She stopped and scanned the garden looking for one particular bush. "Over here."

She drew him to a deep burgundy-leaved bush with strong greenish purple branches and slightly devoid of thorns. On top perched several large buds of red roses nearly halfway opened, revealing a creamy pink-yellow color at the center. She bent over and gave it a sniff.

Trace did the same.

"Wow. Very spicy, but definitely an old rose fragrance," he said.

"You say that like you're an expert."

"Back in Virginia, I actually had a vegetable garden,

if you can believe such a thing."

"Really?" She was fascinated. "You grow them now in San Diego?"

"Nope. I'm in an apartment. Housing's a little more expensive. Back there, I actually had a yard. The married quarters." He winced and rolled his right shoulder then looked to the side, avoiding eye contact.

"Can I ask you about those years, Trace? It's none of my business, of course, but, well, you know a lot about my very public divorce. Was yours like that as well?"

He'd disconnected their handholding and was scanning the horizon with his back to her. When he turned, she saw him grinding his teeth. She wondered if she'd made a mistake.

"You don't have to if you don't want—"

"I'm not very proud of the fact that my divorce was very similar to yours, except the roles were reversed. My ex cheated on me the same way yours did to you. But she not only cheated on me, she did it with another SEAL."

"Someone from your team?"

"Hell no. A sister team. But I did nearly kill him. The dumb sonofabitch should have known better. She'd been my girlfriend ever since we were sixteen in high school. Our dads were both Navy, so we grew up near Norfolk. I never dated anyone else, and I trusted her one hundred percent. Probably more than I'll ever be able to trust again."

He examined his fingers, lacing them and then straightening them out, his body slightly tipping from side to side as if there was a slow dance in the wings somewhere. It moved Gretchen that someone so big and strong could have such a sweet, pure heart. It was something that completely surprised her. The idea that he married his high school sweetheart brought a smile to her face.

"What the Hell are you thinking, Gretchen? Did I say something funny?" he asked. His eyes danced with the banter and play of their conversation.

"Well, I was just thinking that if you only had one girlfriend for all those years—how long were you married?"

"Ten years. We were together nearly fifteen."

"Okay—well, let's just say that I never would have suspected that. You must have made up for lost time." She couldn't hold back her smirk.

"Two years is a long time in Navy years. A lot of trips, missions, countries…"

"I can tell," she whispered.

"Oh, you think so, do you? Well, how about you?" he asked.

A late morning breeze had picked up and kept her cheeks chilly. The sun disappeared behind a fluffy cream and gray cloud, and for a few seconds, the temperature dropped nearly ten degrees. But when the sun returned, she fell into his blue eyes, asking all sorts of questions and giving no permissions.

"Tony has been the only man I've ever slept with. I'm not proud to say that the last years of our marriage, I felt like I was looking over my shoulder all the time to discover who else was in bed with us. After awhile, I just wasn't interested, and I think that's when he really went off the deep end."

Trace stretched out his arms, and she fell into his chest. "You shouldn't ever be made to think you're not desired, Gretchen. A woman shouldn't have to work so hard on herself to get into the mood. That's her man's job."

His comment brought tears to her eyes, but she buried her head in his coat so that he wouldn't see them. As her arms slid around his waist and she held her body against his warmth, she felt safe. The feeling was a strange one for her. For the first time in her life, she really felt cherished.

He held her because he wanted her. He wanted to protect her, because he found her precious. She closed her eyes.

If it's all a dream, don't wake me up. I want to stay here forever.

THE NEXT PLACE she took Trace was Powell's Book Store downtown Portland. "There's a reason they call this Powell's City of Books."

Trace stared at the shelves of books, at the tall ceilings, the catwalks, and little alcoves where hundreds of people milled about, read, and chatted with friends. There was a whole section on Inuit art and culture, something Gretchen was interested in. She had a fairly extensive collection of North Coast Shalish masks adorning her living room walls.

"I'm taking the girls back here in a couple of weeks for some wood carving demonstrations. They have a group of older artisans from British Columbia they're bringing in, to tell stories and talk about their legends. They love it."

"You do a good job with them, Gretchen."

"I just teach them what I like to learn about. They catch on and take it to the next level and start showing me. Having kids keeps me connected with the world. The way I like to read, I'd be holed up in a big chair by the fireplace, reading all day long. But these guys make me get out and learn something about the world we live in."

"Did Tony—"

"Oh, God no. Can't take Tony anywhere. He attracts too much attention. And if he doesn't, he gets uncomfortable and thinks something's wrong."

They ordered an espresso, and Gretchen could see he was impressed with the whole environment.

Test two passed with flying colors.

She leaned on her hands. "So now it's your turn. What would you like to do?"

"I'm enjoying just being here," he said, waving at the two story stacks of shelves and the catwalks switching back and forth. "Coffee's good, and the company is spectacular."

She blushed, unprepared for his answer.

"You read a lot of books?"

Trace frowned. "When I have time. We have downtime, and that's when I read. I don't really read for leisure. I tend to go for science fiction thrillers."

"As if your job wasn't thrilling enough."

Trace cocked his head and winked. "Bingo. But I like the SciFi action, because the spy and military action is a little too close to home, at least when we're on deployment."

"Never figured you for a science fiction kind of reader."

"Oh yea. I'll take aliens any day. Takes my mind off my work sometimes. What do you like to read?"

"You can't guess? With a friend like Linda Gray?"

He smiled in that crooked, sexy way, rubbing his chin stubble and playing with her heartstrings. Did he know he had such an amazing effect on her? Gretchen felt like her whole life was on fire again, blooming, expanding so fast it almost hurt.

"Love stories," he finally said.

"See? That wasn't hard, was it?" Then she added, "We call them romance. And my particular interest is SEAL Romance."

"Like the book with Tyler's abs on the front."

"Exactly. Except I don't see Tyler when I read them. I only see the character Linda writes, not my brother-in-law."

Or maybe now I'll think of you. She knew all that depended on how their few days together went. The real test would be when he returned to San Diego.

Trace smiled and rimmed his coffee cup with his forefinger.

"Okay, I want to know what dirty little thoughts you're having right now Trace. At this café in the middle of the largest book store in the country."

"On deployment, I don't like to read love stories. It's too painful. That's when I go for the pictures. If it's fantasy love, it's gotta have pictures." His return smirk was a challenge. "But I do love to read. Does that qualify?"

You bet it does.

"Well, there's a thought. We could get you your favorite book that has those kinds of pictures, and we could look at it together. What about that?"

"I'm listening." He was rocking on the back legs of the chair again. She leaned forward.

"So what is it, again, you really want to do right now?"

Trace scanned the store like he was looking for something or someone. "How much time do we have?"

Gretchen checked her cell. "After I pick up Angie, the three of us could go somewhere."

Trace finished his espresso and leaned back on his chair. "I was thinking of something more adult. Like a good foreign film. A brew pub. You have lots of them here in Portland."

"How about Italian? There's a theater here where they deliver your pizza while you watch the movie. As far as foreign film, I'm afraid it would have to be a Disney movie."

There was no way in the world she'd have been able to anticipate the answer he gave her.

Trace leaned forward, took her hand, and kissed her palm. "I could do Disney. But I'd love to buy some dirty magazines with you. I'm sure they have them here. And later on, in the privacy of your bedroom, Clover's bedroom, the car, or some other place, what I have in mind is definitely *not* PG."

CHAPTER 16

TRACE HAD IT all planned out. He'd pulled a call to Tyler and Kate and got hold of Tyler's mom, who he knew still lived in Portland. He hoped the surprise was as thrilling to Gretchen as it was to him. He'd had a boner all afternoon, making the arrangements on his cell between Gretchen's errands. He didn't dare tell the girls, but nearly spilled the beans to Angie when she started talking about Kate and Tyler's new baby. He couldn't afford a mishap, so kept silent.

Back at the house, he brought in loads of wood for their wood-burning stove while Gretchen prepared the dinner. He washed clothes and never had such a nice time folding ladies underwear before. He walked out into the dining room holding Gretchen's red bra and panties, unable to slip them on, but holding them in place.

"What to you think? Do I have a chance as an underwear model?" he asked her.

She had just taken a big sip of water and nearly spewed it out over the food she was preparing. Then she had an uncontrollable coughing spasm. He rushed to her side.

"You okay?"

"I can't believe some of the things you think up sometimes, Trace."

It felt so right having her in his arms. He studied the bra and panties on the countertop. "Would you wear these to bed tonight?"

She pulled away and searched his face. "I'd be happy to, as long as you don't compare me to the ladies in those lingerie magazines we bought today."

"They give me ideas, that's all. But you're the one I want to feel naked with."

Their long kiss was interrupted by Angie's frail voice.

"Mom, is Trace a good kisser?"

They immediately dropped their arms, and Gretchen straightened her hair. Trace discretely tucked the underwear into his back pocket.

"Angie, I thought you were upstairs playing in your room." Gretchen's voice broke mid-sentence.

"I heard you laugh, so I came to see what it was about. You guys are funny."

"Where did you pick up that kind of language, Angie? *Good kisser?*" she asked her daughter.

Angie stared at her bare feet. "Clover. She said one of the boys at school was a good kisser." She suddenly realized her mistake and drilled a desperate plea to her mother. "But, Mom! Don't tell her I told you that."

Trace loved Angie's spirit. She was not used to backing down or going away quietly into a corner, and that was a very good thing. Images from his past preoccupied him while Gretchen was giving her little one a gentle lecture on using words that were "too old" for her.

He'd met women who had to fight their whole lives just to survive, to see their children killed on the way to the market or school. He'd seen countries where the fabric of anything that could be called normal life was non-existent. There were thousands of Angies out there who never got the same chances she did.

People didn't understand that coming home after deployments was bittersweet. On one hand, the routine of fighting, waiting, planning, doing dry runs, and more waiting was shattered the first time he stepped off a plane. Wives needed reassurance and attention. They needed to feel loved. Those were the days when he tried to put out of his mind his own needs. It was all about making sure his ex was stable, staying with the program, and still able to be a supportive partner. That kind of firm foundation made for a decent career as a SEAL.

Coming home was also inspiring, just seeing people going about their lives. Walking their dogs, going to church, working in their yards, shopping and finding so much variety. No empty shelves or broken windows. Cars that ran and were clean. House exteriors not marred by missing plaster from a spray of automatic gunfire—an indication of a recent street battle. This was the life they fought to protect. The normal life. The 'just do something and enjoy life.' That's what he was giving his country—the chance to have chances, to have a future that could be planned on.

No sugar-coating it, Trace knew the instant his marriage had changed. It was at a graduation ceremony for the new BUD/S class. Several of their team in Little Creek had come out to California to attend some language training in Monterey, brought the wives, and stayed a long weekend in Coronado to meet the new froglettes. The Team Guy his wife left him for from SEAL Team 4 had a little brother graduating with that class. One thing led to another, and Trace noticed several conversations and smiles that got wiped clean when they saw they were being noticed. There was a champagne toast, then a dinner dance, and a party the next night. All the time he was watching as she fell for the oldest story in the world: a recently divorced, lonely SEAL.

That's when he knew he'd lost her. Before that, he'd

never realized she was even looking. So he understood when Gretchen said she wasn't sure she could trust again. Certainly, Trace felt that way. Would have continued to feel that way all the way through his Hawaii "vacation," if it could be called that, and would have felt okay if it lasted the rest of his life. But in Hawaii, he met Gretchen, and that tilted his whole world on a different axis.

And suddenly, he was surrounded with normal lives that needed protecting—four of them, just doing what they did every day. Eating cereal, visiting a book store, having coffee, drawing pictures, and drinking chocolate milk at school—even talking about "good kissers." It felt great to be able to provide that service to these wonderful people, whether they knew it or not.

Angie walked towards him. "Mom said it was okay that I tell you that *she* says you're a very good kisser." She ran off, giggling. Trace heard her little footsteps traveling up the wooden stairs to her bedroom.

Gretchen had gone back to cooking, but was having difficulty keeping a straight face.

"The apple doesn't fall far from the tree. Not surprised to see little Angie so smart. She'll be a handful when she's Clover's age," Trace said while he wrapped his arms around Gretchen from behind and kissed her neck.

"I refuse to answer that on the grounds it might

incriminate me," she said to the chopped vegetables in front of her.

"Oh, and the punishment is brutal. A hot, sweaty night with a monster who won't leave you alone." His tongue traveled along the arch of her right ear. "I'm gonna make you come—"

"So Tyler's mom's staying for dinner," Gretchen interrupted him with a tease.

Trace dropped his arms and stopped the kissing.

"She'll be here in a few minutes. I was so excited when she offered to pick up the girls from school." Gretchen continued to chop the vegetables, ignoring Trace's heavy-handed come-on.

"That was nice. What a surprise, I'll bet," Trace lied.

"She's very much that way. My mom and dad don't get up here much at all, so she's kind of adopted them."

His boner was killing him.

"Honey, you sure, if we're really fast, we couldn't just have a quickie before the whole house explodes in family? Just a quickie?" he whispered to her ear. "I'll make it worth your while."

"Trace…" She tried to shrug him off. "Would you get that banana out of my butt crack?"

Trace dropped his arms again and stopped kissing her, a little deflated. *He* knew she was preparing a dinner they'd never eat, so of course he wanted to distract her. But he just had to keep the ruse up for a few more minutes. Gretchen was right, but he didn't have to like the reality of it.

"Fine. I look forward to meeting Tyler's mom," he pouted.

Gretchen put the vegetables into a stir-fry pan and left the burner off. She washed her hands with lemon soap and then finally faced him.

"Okay, Romeo. I need you to behave. Watch your language. She's going to be making some evaluations, and she'll give me her opinion, whether I like it or not. I told her you were on the same Team as Tyler. I don't want any awkward moments at the dinner table."

"Promise," he said with his hand over his heart. "You sure we don't have time for that quickie?"

She let out a soft giggle. "I'm sorry about the possibility of your clothing malfunction. You're going to have to hold it a little bit longer."

He stepped forward, pulling her to him. "I'd like you to hold it a little bit longer." He placed her hand over the buttons on his crotch and squeezed.

"Impressive, but nothing, not even a boner the size of Oscar Mayer, will talk me into getting caught doing the dirty with you when Mrs. Gray arrives with my two girls. Nothing. Maybe you should take a cold shower?"

"Man, you're tough."

"Some things are non-negotiable."

"Okay, but don't say I didn't warn you."

She stroked his length, purring like a kitten. "You know that song, *Anticipation?*"

"Don't stop squeezing."

"Making me wait…"

"Harder."

"Think of it as long—" she rubbed up and down, "—very long foreplay."

"Don't stop. I think I dropped something down there, and I can't reach it."

Her breasts were pressed against his chest, her red lips an inch from his. He could feel the warmth of her breath as she whispered, "It will be worth it. I promise."

And then they kissed.

The back door swung wide, and the handle hit the opposite wall, increasing the size of the already existing divot in the sheetrock. Rebecca came skipping in, followed by her older sister. Both the girls had bright smiles and were carrying an overnight case and sheaves of paper.

They must not have noticed that their mother's hand was being led down the front of his pants. Clover blurted out, "Mrs. Gray's going to give us a painting lesson. And she's staying overnight!"

Tyler's mom followed behind. Rebecca ran upstairs with the bag while Clover set the papers down on the table.

"Not there! It's set for dinner, Clover. Put it in the living room."

Heather Gray had a handsome face, salt and pepper long hair pulled into a bun. She wore bright clothes in layers. Her steady eyes examined Trace carefully as she approached in a straight line, full of focus.

"You must be Trace. Nice to meet you. I'm Heather Gray, Tyler's mom."

"Nice to meet you. I've heard good things about you." He tried not to smile too much at the conspiracy he'd created.

Her handshake was firm, and she didn't linger. It was an honest shake. "Forgive me, but, Trace, what's that in your back pocket? Something's sticking out."

Trace had forgotten the red bra and panties. He yanked them quickly and gave them to Gretchen, who discretely stowed them in her apron.

"I was doing laundry this afternoon." He didn't elaborate further and hoped he didn't have to.

Gretchen had begun to turn bright red. Mrs. Gray nodded in recognition. "So you guys are off, then?"

Trace watched Gretchen's expression change from embarrassment to pure surprise.

"Off? I think you got mixed up. I'm making dinner." Gretchen's eyes swept between Mrs. Gray and Trace. "And—and the girls said you're staying overnight?" She focused on Trace, a wrinkle denting her flawless forehead. "Um, we're kind of filled up here, but maybe, if Trace can sleep on the couch, I can give you Clover's room." She'd been looking to Trace to give her a hand.

Mrs. Gray smiled like the wise elder she was. "I think you two better have a little talk. I'll just be upstairs with the girls. We'll be down in a few minutes after you've had your chat, okay?"

Gretchen's eyes were huge. She cocked her head. "Trace, what's going on?"

He was enjoying her confusion. He backed up as she came for him, keeping the distance between them more than arm's length. "I want to know what's going on? What have you done?"

He continued to walk backward as they circled the dining table. "Well, I took the liberty of changing our plans for this evening, and Mrs. Gray said she'd help."

"Change of plans?"

"I booked us a room at the Grover House. And we have reservations at McKinnon's brewpub within walking distance. I thought a nice dinner, just the two of us, and a hotel stay was in order."

"How long have you known about this?"

She still wasn't smiling, and now it started to bother him.

"I planned it today. While you were running those

errands and left me in the car." He stopped moving, and Gretchen reached him, at last. He held her wrists, kissed her palms, and then positioned her arms over his shoulder. "The only choice you have to make is to pick out something to wear tomorrow. We already know you're going to wear that red set tonight, right?"

A smile crept to her lips. Her sparkling eyes and rapid breathing showed her approval of the project he'd planned.

"You're a very clever guy, Mr. Bennett. A little devious, but very clever."

"Oh, you've only seen a small sampling of my arsenal. I can get very creative. The nice thing about this plan is you can make all the noise you want, Gretchen. Now go get your clothes. We don't want to be late for dinner, do we?"

CHAPTER 17

McKinnon's was packed by the time they'd checked into their room and then walked down the rain-drenched street to the brew house. The windows were steamy, and inside, the strong scent of hops and sawdust on the floor added to the ambience of the muggy interior. Gretchen knew Trace would like it.

A duo of guitarists played folk music in the corner.

"How did you decide to come here?" she asked.

"Recommendation by the hotel. I wanted some place where I didn't have to drive. Thought it would be more romantic."

He was right. "I can see how you'd think the smell of beer would be romantic." She winked at him. He grabbed her waist as they were led to their table.

Trace looked over the menu. "No tofu, no bean sprouts or smoothies. I thought Portland was Hippie Central."

"We do have the folk music, but up here, we have a lot of plaid flannel shirts. Where guys hunt and fish and work outside all day, they like their barbeque."

What Trace had noted was the fact that there was either pork or beef in ribs or pulled, potatoes, fresh baked bread slathered with butter, no vegetables, and about thirty varieties of beer. It was a man's menu and not for someone on a diet. She knew he was in Heaven, because he had a hard time making up his mind.

After they ordered, he slipped to the seat next to her. "I'm not going to hear a word you're saying across the table." He gave her a gentle peck on the cheek.

"So what do you think of our fair city?" she asked.

"Interesting. Very different from San Diego. Reminds me of some of the coastal towns back east. Maybe Boston. A little like San Francisco, too, with all the hills." He toasted her, took a long drag off his beer, and smiled. "I can see why you like it. Just a tad cold for me."

"Oh, come on. I've been to Norfolk before. You get some cold, cold winters there. We hardly ever get snow here."

"True. But now that I'm in Southern California, boy, I love it." He paused to study his beer. "You ever visit there?"

"Yes, I've been down to see Kate and Tyler. I'm still a tourist," she answered. She knew he was going to extend an invitation before he said anything at all.

"Best thing to do is to see it through the eyes of someone who lives there. Only been there a few months, but I know all the great spots. And every day it's a pleasant surprise when I find new things I love about it. I'm happy as a clam there."

"I'm glad."

"I'll give you a good time, if you come down and visit. Bring the girls, too, if you want. We've got the zoo, Sea World, all sorts of things."

"Now you're starting to sound like a walking commercial."

Trace shrugged and dropped the invite. "So tell me what you do in Portland that's fun."

"I can tell you don't hang around a lot of mothers of three daughters, Trace. It's just like today, dropping kids off, parent-teacher conferences, ballet, piano lessons, soccer, and volleyball. My day is busy just doing things with or for the girls. That pretty much consumes all my time."

He took her hand and kissed it. "Any space in there for anyone else? Other than vacation, I mean?"

She felt the brakes come on inside. Gretchen wasn't sure where the conversation was headed, and she became cautious.

He sat up, still holding her hand, but sighed and examined their fingers entwined. "I'm sorry if I come on too strong. I do that. I work that way. I play that way."

"Don't feel bad, Trace. You've spent your last few years on a SEAL Team, doing God knows what. I've never been alone. I never get any chance to think about anything, I'm so busy. I'm mom, dad, and taxi driver to those girls. What I want is something I don't have the luxury of thinking about."

The dinner arrived, and they ate in silence. The happy mood that had started their date had now dwindled. They kept their discussion to small talk, and Trace didn't make much eye contact. She thought perhaps he was having second thoughts about the whole evening.

On the way back to the hotel, she leaned her head against his shoulder as they walked. The rain stopped just long enough to get them to the front porch. Inside the old Victorian living room, couples sat by the fireplace. Several others were at the bar. He asked her if she wanted to have a drink, and she declined. It was all polite, and something was definitely wrong.

Inside their room, she sat on the edge of the bed and asked him, "What's going on with you, Trace? Did I say something wrong?"

He hung up his pea coat and washed his hands in the antique lavie. With the towel still in his hands, he faced her, but again didn't make eye contact. "I guess I was just realizing something I hadn't seen before."

"And that is?"

He returned the towel to the bathroom and then sat in a high-backed armchair by the dormered window, bent over, and placed his elbows on his knees, hands clasped. "You're probably going to take this the wrong way, Gretchen. I'm sorry for that, but I'm going to say it, anyway, because I believe we have to be honest with each other."

Gretchen felt her stomach clench up as she held her breath. She had no idea what was coming next. She felt her blood pressure rise. "Go on. I'm a big girl. I can probably handle anything you can say to me."

He smiled to his hands. "Yup. I suppose you're right."

She knew it was the right thing to just wait until he got ready to do it on his terms, but she felt he was going to tell her he wasn't sure their relationship had a future. And that would be okay. She hadn't been looking for that, either. She'd told herself over and over again that it would happen when it was right. Perhaps this just wasn't right.

Trace looked up at her, and she saw something in his eyes she'd never seen before. He had taken off the mask, and she saw real pain there. She resisted the urge to run over to him and mother him.

"What did you realize, Trace? I want to hear it."

"I liked being married, but Shayla broke my heart. I was devoted to her, but in the end, I wasn't enough for her. She left me before she physically did leave. She was looking, and I never picked up on it. Never saw it coming."

"That's horrible."

"No. It's not. She did what she needed to do, and I'm glad she did, because although I thought we were happy, we really weren't. We could have spent even more years pretending to have a life. Hell, I wouldn't have known the difference. I mean, if a person can fool you into thinking they love you and then they walk out—I mean, we never argued. And I didn't even put up a fight to keep her. I just let her go."

"Maybe it wasn't meant to be. Maybe you were logical about it. I don't think that's a bad thing."

She studied his face. Was he asking her something or making a statement? She couldn't read what was going on inside him.

"I think what scares me is that I *liked* it, being married. I've not had a serious relationship since. I'm afraid I'm not good at that sort of thing."

"What do you mean? What sort of thing?"

"You know, I wanted someone who could feel for me like I felt for her. And man, that sounds twisted and sick. But I don't want to be a secondary character. I want to be prime time. And you—"

She felt hot tears well up.

"You are devoted—*have* to be devoted—to your daughters. Just listening to you talk about the girls and your life, I don't think there is anything left over for anyone else. You're being a great mom and a great role model. It's unfair of me to even think of inserting myself into that life or, worse yet, taking you away from all that. It would be like you asking me to leave the Teams."

He was right, of course. Maybe they'd jumped in too deep too fast. Now that they were looking at themselves honestly, there was more to what they really wanted than just great sex. She saw that perhaps she wouldn't be able to be the woman he needed, like it would be nearly impossible for him to be the kind of man she and her girls wanted. If she was single, it would be totally different. But she wasn't. She had three girls, and they had as much say as she did in the matter.

But as she examined her insides, another thought occurred to her.

"Don't you think two people can have a relationship and still be fully devoted to other things? Other family members or careers like yours? Not other life partners, but isn't there a part of us that admires the devotion it takes to do what I do, to do what you do?

He was silent, and then he nodded. "Gretchen,

you're a wise woman. That fits. That's who we are. We have that in common."

Rain started misting outside, getting heavier and heavier until it was pouring. Trace closed the window to stop the sill from getting wet. She scanned the beautiful, antique-furnished room, the happy surprise he sprung on her where they could talk, have dinner together, and anticipate a night of wonderful sex. He'd planned it all out and did it for both of them. It was a beautiful gesture and not to be wasted, though perhaps there wasn't that silver lining or sunshine on the other side of the mountain.

She'd made a decision.

She walked to the chair, grasping his hands in hers, motioning for him to stand up. She placed her palms on his chest then felt the sandpaper sides of his leathery face. Saw the pain in his eyes and felt the beating of his heart.

"I have a suggestion, Trace. See if this will work for you. Let's pretend for this one night that we are both new at love. Let's pretend we've never been married, hurt, or had children. Let's pretend for tonight that this one evening will be perfect. Tomorrow, it doesn't have to mean anything. We don't have to analyze it or understand its meaning. Let's just pretend that no one has ever hurt us before, that the slate has been wiped clean."

His hands came to her face as he lifted her chin and bent down to kiss her. A second before his lips touched hers, he murmured, "I can do that. If you'll help me."

The kiss was long and unhurried. She explored all the colorful emotions the touch of his mouth on hers brought. She imagined pictures of places she'd never seen before and felt the lightness in her chest as he slipped his fingers around to the back of her head and sifted through her hair. He was a brick wall, solidly packed so hard that the tenderness in his kiss, his fingers, and how he held her in his fragile way moved her. She could help him by going the rest of the distance, meeting him in the middle. He melted the layers of self-preservation and caution. He turned her bones to rubber with each kiss.

Their kissing became a slow disrobing, clothes strewn where they lay. Only her red bra and panties were left on her. She stepped closer to touch the length of his body, felt his powerful thighs and tight butt, let her fingers travel over the scars of his life's work. And although he'd wanted her to wear the set, she decided she didn't even want the barrier of the thin silky fabric between them. She slipped out of her panties and removed her bra, presenting herself to him completely naked. She wasn't one of the pinup girls in the magazine. She had a woman's body, had borne three children, carried scars the same as he, because this was her life's work. But she would give him that body honestly.

He remained slow and reserved, playing her so finely, attuned to what she wanted, that she began to spin out of control, found herself calling his name and begging for more.

His pace quickened like a gradual wave that could go on forever. His lips kissed and sucked her nipples; his tongue devoured her. His thumb pressed her bud as he furiously stroked her insides. The long, rolling orgasm had begun at last, making it impossible to hold on, but she still tried. She was slipping, slipping into the warm abyss, and still she wanted more.

"Let go, Gretchen. Take me with you," he whispered.

Her muscles slammed against his. She tore herself from under him and climbed atop, pushing down with his cock buried deep inside her. She was a wild woman, a female she'd only dreamt about. He gripped her buttocks hard, and she felt herself squeeze down on him, making him jump. As he began to come, he wrapped his powerful arms around her, nearly squeezing the breath out of her, holding her on his lap at the edge of the bed, forcing himself deeper still until both their bodies began to shudder in unison.

She was wrung out. Her chin rested on his massive shoulder. Sweat trickled down his spine. His fingers found the wet hair at the back of her neck as he pulled it aside, and he kissed her there. The scent of sex and unbridled desire filled her nostrils and made her want to come all over again.

She barely had the energy to turn her head. She bit his ear lobe, their bodies breathing together heavily, and she whispered, "I don't want this to stop."

His deep grumble and groan gave her a flash of energy as he pumped his pelvis up, lifting her body impaled on his cock.

"Baby, I can do this all night. I don't think I *can* stop."

She leaned back to see his face in the moonlight. Glistening beads of sweat coated his forehead and the sides of his cheeks. His full lips were soft to the touch as she brought her fingers up to feed his mouth and then feel their joining tongues.

Picking her up, he brought her into the shower, turning on the warm water, letting it wash over her burning body. He pressed her against the cool tile wall, lifted her right leg behind the knee, let his fingers explore her channel and pinch her nub, then guide his thick member home. Her fingers tried to grip the smooth, wet surface of the tiled wall. She angled her pelvis back, begging him to fill her. His pumping action brought tears to her eyes as she moaned and cried out.

Her body was electric with the need of this man. She muffled her voice, pleading against the wall, desperate for him.

His words, whispered so sweetly in her ear, made her insides explode.

"I'm here, baby. Not going to leave you. Not *ever* going to leave you, baby."

CHAPTER 18

TRACE SLEPT VERY little. When he wasn't fully consumed with the touch and feel of Gretchen's smooth flesh as he made love to her over and over again, he watched her sleep, held her against him, and did what she asked. He pretended he'd never been hurt. That he'd never known the heartache of a love blown or fading away. He felt more and more possessive of her the more he fed from the sexual energy she gave back to him. She was strong, but pliable. She was female, but not fragile. She was a free spirit, giving up the secrets of the rhythm she liked, what she wanted to feel, and how he could please her. Unashamed. Even the way she'd slipped off her panties and bra told him she had bared her soul to him.

It wasn't a mere fantasy. The lovemaking was more than sex. It was communion, a bridge between two hearts starved for one another. The rest of the world, true to her wish, was a universe away.

He mentally pushed the sun back under the horizon, tried to stop the new dawn from breaking through, because he wasn't done loving her, and he didn't want her to go back to her other life. In this room, in this big bed, he was master of her body, and she had enslaved him in the golden rings of pleasure she brought to him. The more he took, the more he wanted.

She stirred, her thigh slipping over his, her sweaty sex breathing against his flesh as if it was begging to be fed one more time. He'd do it, when he got good and ready to. But, for now, he wanted to look at her face, her eyes closed, her tongue licking her lips as she crawled up his thigh, pressing herself against him, and then shifting herself down again. As she breathed, her breasts made wet pools on his chest. Her blonde hair darkened against her face. His fingers pulled her hair back and off her forehead, where he kissed her, then inched down to plunge his tongue deep inside her mouth. Her satisfying gasp told him he'd pierced her veil of sleep and once again she was his to command.

"Trace," she mumbled.

He kissed under her chin to let her finish. "Tell me. Right here, baby."

"Don't stop, Trace."

"I don't intend to, sweetheart."

He rolled her to her stomach, pulled a pillow under

her, folding it in half and elevating her sweet butt. All too tempting, he touched her hot core, pressed two fingers inside her, and felt the vibration of her deep moan into the pillow.

"You like that, baby?"

"Trace—Oh God, Trace!"

"Right here, baby."

He bent, kissed both butt cheeks, and then slipped his tongue inside her opening, adding a thumb, then a finger, then two as she writhed beneath him.

Her hand came around to grip his arm and pulled slightly, asking that he ride her from behind.

"You like this, baby?" he said as he got to his knees, spread her cheeks, and watched his cock tease the pink lips of her sex. She was raising herself to accept him, and he was withholding until she needed him even more. Her forlorn moans nearly broke his heart.

"Please," she begged.

"I'm going to fix it. I have what you need, baby."

"Yes! Please."

He placed his crown at her opening and very deliberately inserted himself, stopping on each of her moans, kissing her cheeks. The feel of her swollen lips squeezing his girth and their combined juices was delicious when he tasted his fingers. He pinched her bud gently, rolling it around between his third finger and thumb, and then gently pulled. He felt the stretched opening of her channel and rimmed it with his fingers.

He pressed himself inside her and then held her pelvis up with one hand on her belly, gently raising the angle, pulling her onto him so he could plunder deeper still.

Her shoulder muscles rippled under her sweaty flesh. While fully seated, he could feel the spasms inside her milking him, begging him to spill. He kissed the back of her neck and swept aside her sweaty hair. He arched back to angle deep again, then leaned back, pulled her right thigh up and over in front of him, turning her onto her side, and fucked her at an angle, the delicious feel of flesh coating his member. His hands fondled her breasts. He watched her dazed eyes yearn for him to play her further.

He took her right hand, and together, they massaged his balls, traced the liquid outline of her opening, and then fed her the juices they'd made.

"Oh God," she cried suddenly as she began to orgasm.

He flipped her onto all fours and furiously pumped her, her breasts overflowing in his hands. She grabbed the metal headboard tightly as he released himself to her.

The morning sun gave gentle warmth, their bodies glowing against the white hotel sheets. They lay facing each other, watching each other's eyes until their breathing allowed speech.

"You're incredible, Gretchen," he said, still catching his breath.

"You make me incredible, Trace. I never knew sex could be like this. It's like—"

He answered her smile with one of his own. "Like we're brand new at this, discovering sex for the first time."

She nodded. "Like wiping the slate clean."

He dared not say anything more, because the night and now this morning were perfect. There would be time enough to let the real world come calling.

HE WAS STARVED for a big breakfast. Gretchen smiled the whole time while they walked to the restaurant. She hardly touched her food, but avidly watched him shovel it in.

"What time did you tell her we'd be home?" she asked.

He fed her pancakes dripping with syrup. "God, I love those lips. Do you suppose those lips could—?"

"More coffee?" the perky waitress asked, holding up her round little pot half the size of her oversized boobs.

They both nodded, chuckling, and accepted the hot liquid.

"I'd give anything to see her expression if she'd really heard you," Gretchen began. "But what I'd really like is to have you finish your sentence."

She was blushing.

"I'm game." Trace moved to sit in the booth closer to her. "I was wondering if those lips," he continued as he fed her another forkful of pancakes, "would suck my dick when we get back to the hotel."

"So Mrs. Gray doesn't have to be back right away, then."

"I told her noon. She said she was going to give them a painting lesson somewhere downtown, and then we'd meet her at your house at noon." He kissed her syrup-drenched lips. "Hmmm. You taste good."

She quickly scanned the room as if making sure no one she knew would hear her. "Then I'd probably have time to suck your dick. Maybe twice."

He liked that she played along. "Now why didn't I think of that? That would be perfect. I think I could be persuaded to make you scream my name again."

Gretchen was still smiling when they left the restaurant.

"I like your smile, baby," he whispered as they walked casually toward the hotel.

"You made that smile," she answered and squeezed his hand.

Confident and content, he nodded in agreement.

Yes. He. Did.

CHAPTER 19

IT WASN'T UNTIL Trace had boarded the plane that Gretchen let down the gates and allowed the rest of her world to come crashing in. The girls had been great those last two days Trace was with them. He didn't overplay it or make a fool of himself. He showed his genuine interest in them. If it was an act, it was a very good one.

Every once in a while, she'd catch him watching her from across the room, and when their eyes connected, she felt that same thrill she felt the first time she kissed him. But those were few and far between. Daytime was filled with activities involving the girls, and the nights, those breathless nights, were made for love. There was never a time they could sit down and just have a long talk. She knew he missed that as well. So his leaving left a lot of things undecided and unfinished.

A part of her wondered if the distance between

them or lack of constant rubbing up against one another would make their fondness grow cold.

Does that happen when the girls go off to camp or go visit their grandparents? Then why am I worried about this?

She didn't push for a commitment, still unsure she could trust herself, recalling that discussion they'd had when Mrs. Gray came to babysit. Though he acted casual and relaxed, she knew he was good at masking his emotions. It was way too soon for talk of a long term plan. They were still getting to know each other. And part of her worried they'd been thrown together with Clover's kidnapping. If that hadn't happened, they wouldn't have connected as strongly as they did. Under stress and crises, people formed bonds they wouldn't otherwise. She didn't trust herself.

Instead of feeling sad that he was leaving, she was filled with uncertainty. He hadn't volunteered a promise nor had she given him one. They didn't even have a time they would get together again, and he'd stopped asking her for a visit down to Coronado.

Tony and Joanie were at the house with the kids when she returned from the Portland Airport. She expected Joanie, but with Tony in tow and the girls sitting in a row on the couch with their hands folded and their legs crossed in the same direction and Clover's face looking like she'd been crying, Gretchen knew something was up.

Setting down her shoulder bag, jacket, and keys, she accepted Tony's peck on the cheek after she walked over to them all. Tony sat back down and Joanie, who had also stood, had missed her chance to give her a hug or a handshake, which would have been weird.

Angie cast her glance down, but kept her chin up, trying to maintain a certain demeanor. Rebecca looked the same as normal.

"So, Gretchen, I understand your SEAL boyfriend left today. I would have liked to thank him for what he did for Clover," Tony started. It was also unlike him to be so nice.

"He's not my boyfriend, Tony. He's a good friend."

Angie inhaled and was about to say something, and Gretchen stopped her with that look she could give the girls. She knew the little one was going to say something about how he was a good kisser, since this delicious new piece of vocabulary crept into nearly every discussion these days.

Clover winced, her right eye in a fluttery spasm. She looked uncomfortable.

"Well, there's time for that later, I suppose. I'm sure you'll find someone really worthy some day."

Again, Tony's demeanor was off. Joanie grabbed his enormous hand and wove her fingers around his. It looked like an act of encouragement.

"You guys want anything to drink?" She had been looking at Tony and Joanie, but all three of the girls answered. "Yes, Mom."

"You two stay put, and Clover come with me to help out. Tony? Joanie?"

Joanie said yes, but he said no.

"Just water, please, Gretchen. Don't go to any trouble," Joanie said sweetly.

Without asking, Gretchen filled two short glasses and four taller glasses with ice from the freezer door and cool water. She whispered to her oldest, "Give these to your dad and Joanie. I'll take these for you and your sisters. And thank you, honey."

"I don't like being around her, Mom," Clover whispered back. "Will I have to stay with them more, now that they're—"

Clover stopped, suddenly aware of something she almost said and wasn't supposed to. Gretchen was beginning to understand Tony's reason for stopping by on a game day.

"Is that what this's about?"

The small-talk background conversation in the living room had ended and was still. *Too* still.

Clover's eyes drooped, and her forehead wrinkled. "Can they take me away from you?"

Panic sparked through Gretchen's body. This had completely taken her out of her idyllic mood, with the taste and the memory of Trace still on her lips—the man who made her feel whole and safe. Now she would have to face this demon alone.

"We'll discuss it later in private. Don't worry. No one's going to take you away, ever, without your approval, Clover."

Her hands shook slightly, holding the four glasses including one for herself. She wanted to touch Clover's cheek, but instead followed her into the living room.

Tony's timing was pretty good, just like it always was. She was without her backup, and she'd not had time to prepare, mentally.

She handed the glasses to her girls, requesting they scoot aside so she could sit between Clover and Angie, and then carefully took a sip of water and waited.

Tony downed his in one gulp. "Gretchen, Joanie and I are planning a June wedding. We'd like the girls to be very involved."

Gretchen knew there was more, but she vowed not to let a single crack in her granite exterior to show.

"That would be fun," she said. As she looked at each of the girls, they all nodded. "You'd have a good time with that, wouldn't you?" Rebecca and Angie were polite and nodded with wide smiles. Clover was sullen.

And then the other shoe dropped. "Gretchen, Joanie and I were talking, and we'd like the girls stay with us half the time at first. But perhaps it could be made into a permanent arrangement later on, if you wanted some freedom. You've worked so hard these past years, scraping together the money to keep the house, and I know you must be exhausted. I'm giving you the chance to go live your life. Travel. Have fun."

Gretchen hadn't realized she hated Tony as much as she did. Every ounce of respect and care she had for the man had been reduced to the size of a fly she was about to step on.

Tony was about to give another reason why his proposal was a good idea when Gretchen stopped him.

"Tony, shut up. The girls *are* my family. They are not a burden. They are my pride and joy. And even if it were true, how dare you say these things in front of them? I would never consider sharing custody with you."

"Well, the law has changed, and fathers now have rights." Tony was getting his hackles up, working into an angry phase she knew all too well. "Before, I was single. But now I'm getting married. And, let's face it, I can more afford to take care of them than you can. I'm the right choice."

"Except have you asked the girls what they want?" Gretchen asked.

"I just mentioned it today. They have a while to think about it."

"*Think* about it? This isn't a unilateral decision,

Tony. You can't just waltz in here and decide you want to do this. It's not fair to me, and it's certainly not fair to them."

"Oh sure, poison them against me, like you always do."

The argument continued for several minutes. Gretchen worked to stay calm, but Tony was near boiling point.

The girls looked very somber, heads bobbing between their mother and then following their father's retorts. Joanie was caught in the middle. Gretchen was grateful she had her arms around the girls, because it reminded her that they were the most important people in the room. The argument wasn't really about she and Tony. It was about the girls and the impact this would have on their lives.

Tony wasn't considering them for a second.

"I'm calling a break here, Tony. No more. If we're going to have this discussion, it's going to be in private. And since we can't seem to be civil to each other, perhaps we should have someone else do it," she said.

"I'm fine with that," he said, slamming down his glass on her coffee table. "I've got the best attorneys in the State of Oregon. And I happen to know you struggle to even pay your phone bill. Gretchen, who do you think's going to come out ahead?"

She stood. "I want you and Joanie to leave. This is

not happening in front of the girls." She reached down and spoke to them in a whisper, "Please go upstairs, and I'll be there when they leave."

The girls filed by their company one at a time, and as they were climbing the bannister, Tony blurted out, "Not so much as a hug or goodbye?"

Little courageous Angie was the only one to stop, turn to him, and say, "Goodbye, Daddy." Then she ran up the steps to catch up with her sisters and disappeared.

Gretchen studied the way Joanie tried to calm him down, like a butterfly flitting all over the place. Gretchen knew she'd have to learn to become much more adept at coping with his anger, or she'd get the back of his hand eventually, like Gretchen did twice. She'd been a fool to not leave then and there. But all that was in the past. And it had been hard for the family to understand how emotionally weak Tony really was. The whole world looked at him like a celebrity, a super hero who could do no wrong. And in that environment, he never had to come to grips with the pain he inflicted on everyone around him.

Tony was nearly out the door before Joanie realized he was leaving. "I'm sorry, Gretchen. I don't know why he had to tell you about his plans for the girls. This was supposed to be a special day, asking for his girls to be in the wedding. I didn't know he was going to behave this way."

"Joanie, you're in for a very long row to hoe. It will never get easier. In fact, I think he's gotten worse."

"Maybe if we have a baby, it will settle him down."

Gretchen couldn't believe her ears. The woman standing before her was actually considering having a baby with that man. She was going to say something to her when they both heard Tony's car horn.

"Be careful, Joanie. Take good care of yourself and watch your back. I mean it."

Gretchen noted her surprised expression as Joanie fumbled for her purse, turned around, and then headed out the front door onto the porch and the stairs down below.

She was so glad she was out of that snake pit as she watched them drive off. But the looming storm clouds on the horizon and possible attorney's fees, which she could not afford, worried her.

She checked and locked the downstairs doors and windows, removed the glasses from the living room, and then ascended the wooden stairway. The air had been sucked out of her lungs. She couldn't even remember what it felt like to laugh or to be held, protected by someone who cared for her. Even Trace's face blurred. Linda Gray had been right. She was so starved for that kind of affection after having been denied it for so long, she'd do almost anything to get it back.

But tonight she had a job to do. There would be no crying herself to sleep or reading a good book to take her mind off her troubles. She had three little angels to protect from this monster called their father. If she wasn't clear-headed, she'd make a mistake that could cost them all dearly. She had to be brave and tough for them.

Her happily ever after would have to come later.

CHAPTER 20

TRACE GOT BACK to Coronado just in time to walk into a SEAL Team 3 meeting.

Tyler gave him a shake and a slap on the back.

"Glad you could make it, Trace," his LPO, Kyle Lansdowne said by way of greeting. "Everything right as rain?"

"One hundred percent."

"How's the little one doing?"

"Tough as nails, like her mom."

Armando barked, "Uh-oh, she cut you off?"

"Didn't mean it that way," Trace tried to whisper, but the room erupted in shouts anyway.

"I'm sure you heard, but I'll go over it one time for clarity. Their vacation was cut short by the kidnapping of Tyler's niece. Trace, Coop, Armando, and Fredo flew to Portland and foiled what was going to be a botched ransom demand. Saved the little girl's life."

Appreciative nods and mumbling of praise sounded amongst the Team.

"Clover was—what?—fourteen?" Kyle squinted and cocked his head.

"Yup."

"Okay, so show and tell is over. And we're back to focusing on the really big shit." Lansdowne paced the sanded concrete floor. "We need to start planning the next deployment, coming up very soon now."

The room fell silent.

He stopped in front of Trace and barked, "You're the newest guy on the team. We got no special favors just because you happen to have been a hero last week. We got a room full of heroes. You, my man, are in charge of the Team's Honeypot."

The room erupted into a roar.

He wasn't sure, but he guessed it was the Team's stash of porn that traveled with them wherever they went.

"Is it any good?" he asked. He heard ripples of laughter.

Armando answered him. "So when you hear Trace is taking too much time in the bathroom, you'll know what he's doing."

"Don't feel bad, Trace," Ollie added. "Most the magazines are light on account of the pictures being torn out you actually don't have much to pack."

"Then I'll add a few of my favorites."

Everyone laughed.

"Okay, listen up. We're going to be heading to the Caribbean this time, but this ain't no picnic," Kyle started. "We're landing at an old church campground on St. Croix the US Government recently bought for these types of ops. We'll be building things as part of our "training," and our cover is that we're a bunch of Seabees setting up a military training camp. That also gives us the excuse to explore the island and not carry heavy weapons, but trust me, we'll have them. Don't want anything like what happened to us in Mexico last time."

"So that's the job? Don't we have a target?" asked Tyler. "And any idea how long we'll be gone?"

"Oh, we got a target all right. We got a dude living on a houseboat, but it's not like anything you'd see in the swamps of Louisiana. It's a converted small cruise ship. His own private paradise, flying a pirate flag. He entertains, has a casino, and lots of babes, but he rents rooms. Like a floating hotel. It's sort of a loss leader for him. He's looking for the big guys to buy his drugs."

"He's American?" asked T.J.

"From St. Croix. We also think he runs girls. He comes into port one day, and several girls go missing the next, never to be seen again. We aim to take him down, eventually. This is the first part. Set up the base camp."

AFTER THE MEETING broke up, Trace followed some of the other Team Guys over to the Rusty Scupper for some beers. He learned one of the Team's "retired" SEALs was going to make a run and try to come back.

"It's been done before," said Lucas. "That tat guy did it. Was out ten years and then went back."

"Yeah, Kirby North," nodded Fredo. "Helluva guy. He ran with the Angels during those ten years. Can you imagine that?"

Trace had heard of this guy and vowed he'd like to shake the man's hand. It would mean that he would be coming back to the teams ten years from now. That took a lot of guts.

The group broke up and called it a night. Trace called Gretchen, but didn't get an answer. Then he looked at the clock, and it was past ten-thirty before they left the Scupper.

Should have called her earlier. Damn.

"Hey, Gretchen, got here safe and sound and had to hightail it to the Team building for our Com report. Tyler says hi, by the way. I'll call you in the morning. Hope I didn't wake you." He hesitated, but ended the call with, "Missing you already, baby."

When he returned to his apartment, he dropped his bag inside the door and stared at his sorry place. He had a beat-up leather couch he'd bought at the local Crossing Jordan store, and it looked like hell. His big screen TV was on a stack of five pallets, which took up a lot of space, but since he didn't have any other furniture in there, it was no problem. The colorful part was the nudie posters. He'd collected his favorites over his five years of bachelorhood. The parade of fleshy and flimsy stuff extended into his single bedroom. His king-sized bed was the only truly awesome thing in his place.

One of the guys had asked him why he didn't have more stuff, since he'd been married. He told them he'd let Shayla take everything. And what she didn't take, he threw away. He didn't want anything left to remind himself of her in any way, shape, manner, or form.

But the inside of his apartment, where he didn't spend a whole lot of time, mimicked the insides of his love life. At least until a week ago, when he'd met Gretchen in Hawaii. Oh, yes, it had been fun to buy those magazines at the book store in Portland, but those were tame compared to the ones he had piled up beside his bed and stuffed into shelves in his coat closet.

But now he had a real coat to hang there. She'd let him take the Navy pea coat, which he removed and put on a lone, bent wire hangar. He took out a stack of magazines and set them in the hallway outside his door. The teenagers in the complex would find them before the janitor did.

He walked around the room and ripped the posters off the wall, some twenty of them. It wasn't that he'd changed, really. He was moving on. Just like in his marriage to Shayla, he didn't want anything to remind him of those lonely years being heartbroken.

He brought his duty bag into the bedroom and took out a pair of his boxers. It was too warm in Coronado for the long pajama bottoms he wore in Portland. Slipping off his clothes, he tossed them in the closet with his other dirty clothes and took a long, steamy shower.

He wanted a beer, although he'd had more than a couple at the Scupper shooting the shit with the other guys. But the refrigerator was bare, and he didn't feel like getting dressed and visiting the convenience store down the street. He decided it would be best to just go to bed.

Caribbean. Wow. He'd been there several times when he and Shayla could catch those cheap direct flights. Loved all the bright colors and the white beaches. Hawaii was lush and old school beautiful. He wanted to go back and thought perhaps Gretchen might like a second vacation, since the first one had been marred by the kidnapping.

But the Caribbean was some place he never thought he'd go as a SEAL. There had to be some government angle going on to bring in the SEALs.

Perhaps some Senator's daughter got caught up with this cretin or something. More would be revealed, no doubt. Why would the US Government want to disrupt a crazy guy selling drugs off a houseboat? Wasn't that something for the locals and, closer to home, for the Coast Guard?

But sure, he'd take the blue waters and steel drum music. He'd take his share of rum, too.

He turned off the bedside light and settled down when his cell rang.

"Sorry I missed your call, Trace," Gretchen said, breathless like she'd been running. "I was reading to the girls and then doing laundry. Hope it's not too late."

"No, sweetheart, your timing is perfect. Just tucked myself into bed, and as a matter of fact, I was thinking of you."

He knew she was smiling.

"I had a rough encounter with Tony tonight. Don't want to get into it, but just needed to hear your voice again."

"What happened?"

"It's too much to go into right now. I'm exhausted. We were all upset. In a nutshell, though, Tony is getting married in June and has asked the girls to be in the wedding."

"Okay." Trace wasn't sure why this would cause so

much upset, unless Gretchen harbored more feelings for Tony than she let on.

"And he's visiting his rights as a future married man, as far as the girls go. He's thinking of taking me to court over it."

"Oh, damn. That's totally fucked. What an asshole."

"We'll sort it out. I've talked to my mom, and she gave me the name of a good attorney who specializes in custody cases. I just hope he's not too expensive. But I'll be fine."

"And who knows? He spends a couple of weeks with all three of them, Tony's likely to send them back home. At least that's what I imagine him to be like."

"It isn't anything to do with the girls. It's about punishing me, taking them away from me."

"Gotta hope a judge would see right through that."

"Except for one thing, Trace. Tony is a Portland icon. Nobody would ever believe me if I told them how he treated me and the girls."

"Have more faith, Gretchen. Wish I could go with you to the wedding, as your backup, but I'll be on deployment."

"I was afraid of that. When do you leave?"

"Not supposed to say, but we're not sure, anyhow."

"Will you be far?"

"Can't say that, either, sweetheart. Sorry. But more

than likely I'll be gone in June and probably July as well. I'll be in phone contact, though, occasionally."

"At least we'll have that."

The silence between them was awkward, so he told her to get some rest and plot everything out she needed to do in the morning when she felt fresh.

"Already done that."

"You work fast."

"When things are jumbled, I obsessively plan. It's a weakness, I guess."

"Hell no to that. That's a strength here on the Teams. Planning is everything."

"Well, I'll let you get some rest, and I promise to double check all my lists in the morning when I'm fresh. I'm going to miss not cuddling up to you to-night."

"Me, too, baby. You call me anytime. Anytime you need to talk. And don't worry about anything. It will all turn out. I'll give you a call tomorrow if I can. But I'll definitely call you before we leave."

"Thanks, Trace." After a pause, she said, "Good night."

"Good night, Gretchen."

They hadn't said the "L" word yet, so the sign-off felt a bit abrupt.

But that's just the way it is.

As he watched the patterns of light flash across his

ceiling, he wondered what kind of man could father three precious girls, and care so little for their welfare. The man didn't deserve the gift he'd been given.

He was also clear about something else. It wasn't his place to step into the man's shoes. The dynamics of this family, although he cared about them all, was not something he should get involved with. Good or bad, the girls had a father. He wasn't going to steal the man's chance to redeem himself and make a fresh start.

No matter how unlikely it was.

CHAPTER 21

"MOM. DOES DADDY love us?" Angela asked her.

"Of course he does," Gretchen explained. "He shows it differently than I do or Grandma does, than just about everyone."

She could have the talk about his being selfish with Clover, but with Angie and Rebecca, she'd risk one of them saying something to him, and that could set him off.

Clover said nothing about their interchange. When the girls weren't invited to Tony's weekend game, which had been the custom, they all relaxed. Gretchen wasn't looking forward to another confrontation. Every day the mailman came, she was nervous to perhaps find a Summons.

The attorney that Tyler's mom used dealt with intellectual property rights for artists. Heather had some choice words to describe Tony's outburst, especially doing so in front of the three girls.

"The guy's had everything handed to him. He's a freak of nature. But that doesn't hold any standing with me. He could do with less muscle mass and more common sense," Heather Gray told her.

"I'm hoping he'll get so involved in the wedding that he'll forget the whole thing," answered Gretchen.

"You really think so? Seems to me he wants what he wants and doesn't matter who it cuts across. Poor Joanie. I hope you warned her, discretely, of course."

"I did. I'm not going to tell you what she said as a response."

"You have to tell me now."

"She thinks if they have a child together it will settle Tony down."

"Oh God, one of those."

"Don't get me wrong, children are a blessing. But to use them to patch up a flawed marriage? It's not fair to the child. I was so naive and so enamored with Tony's charisma I didn't see all that."

"You've done a great job, Gretchen. I'll think about a referral, ask around. In my crowd, though, most everyone is grandparents. But I'll keep asking. You want a pit bull."

Gretchen laughed. "That's for sure. If you have a pit bull on Tony's ankle, doesn't matter how tall he is."

Later in the week, she managed a phone conversation with the attorney her mother recommended in

Palo Alto.

"Is there any dispute with the paternity?"

Gretchen was taken aback. "Excuse me?"

"Well, could any of these girls not be his daughter?"

"Of course not!" She looked into the phone as if it had been crawling with ants.

"Just had to ask. So both of you acknowledge Tony is the biological father."

"Yes."

"And he's not paid any child support, even though he's an NBA star?"

"I refused the money. I told him instead to put it in a fund for their college, which he's done."

"You could go after him for back child support," he suggested.

"But that doesn't solve the problem of the custody of the girls. I'm not interested in making him mad. I just want to keep the girls, and I don't want them spending lots of time over there. It isn't a good environment. Joannie's inattention led to my daughter being kidnapped!"

"A judge might not agree with you. Think of the things Tony can provide that you cannot. I'm not agreeing with this at all, but you can see how someone on the outside might construe it differently."

"They don't need to live in a palace and be driven to school with a driver to have a normal life. They need love and care. A parent who will spend time with them."

After the discussion, Gretchen was worried. Tony had deeded the house over to her, such that she could make the payments on her own. They'd put over fifty percent down, from one of Tony's bonuses. And in exchange, she didn't take any money from him for support, because of pride. She'd been discarded, traded in on a new model. And before this week, he'd never seemed interested in maintaining a relationship with the girls.

The following week, Joanie asked to have coffee with her to discuss the wedding plans.

"I appreciate you doing this, Joanie," Gretchen said as she arrived at the coffee house. "I don't want to discuss all this in front of the girls."

Joanie was already sipping her latte. "I thought it would be best," she said meekly. "Go get your coffee. I'll wait."

Gretchen scanned the room, filled with college and high school students doing their homework or working on computers. Joanie's ponytail was just as bouncy as it was two weeks ago, but something caught her eye. On the left side of Joanie's neck was a sizeable bruise. She'd flipped up her pink jogging suit jacket, but on the left side, the collar had turned down, revealing the bruise.

It had always been at the back of her mind that if

she remained with Tony, he'd eventually be physical with her. The first time he slapped her across the face, she'd been filled with shock, and could not believe it. She expected he'd feel horrible and collapse and hold her, but instead, he was furious. "*You made me do this.*"

He'd been drinking, so she chalked it up to that. But when it happened the second time, she knew something was wrong. Seeing the pictures on TV with the half-naked dancer only confirmed the fact that Tony was going through some kind of melt down. Everything became Gretchen's fault. Even the girls needing her attention was a criticism. The tighter Tony seemed to grip, the more elusive their relationship became. She'd finally had enough when Clover saw the spectacle on TV that she knew she had to get out.

Luckily, he never resisted. She figured he was too preoccupied with all the publicity and attention he was getting. A divorce was what every bad boy was destined for, and he seemed to accept and even like it.

Gretchen brought her cup to the table.

"I have to ask you something. Has Tony been violent with you, Joanie?"

The gorgeous Barbie Doll furled her eyebrows together and curled her lip.

"No. Why would you ask me that?"

"Because of that." She pointed to the left side of

Joanie's neck. "That's a bruise your makeup can't hide."

"Oh, that!" She laughed, making light of it. "We were wrestling, you know. On accident, I came down on the edge of the coffee table. Just a harmless accident."

She delivered it smoothly, but the way Joanie searched Gretchen's eyes gave her away. She searched for evidence Gretchen had fallen for the ruse. Gretchen thought it was unwise to divulge that Tony had hit her twice. But she wanted to warn the woman, if she'd hear her. She decided it was too dangerous.

Gretchen changed the subject and let Joanie describe what she had in mind for the special day. The two younger girls would spread rose petals ahead of the bride. Clover could be one of the bridesmaids.

They looked over dresses and the reception hall, adjacent to the old Episcopal church. It was going to be a very expensive and beautiful affair.

"I can't wait to see all this unfold, Joanie. When Tony and I got married, he wanted to elope. My mother really read him the riot act and insisted on something. But I'm glad you're doing it this way, and how fun for the girls to be involved."

"You think so? I was worried about that."

"It's more awkward for Clover. But Angie doesn't even remember when Tony lived with us. We had very little money at first. Life was simple. I didn't mind. But if you can, well, why not have a big grand wedding?"

"Thank you. I'm really glad you approve. My parents can't afford this, so Tony's paying for all of it." She beamed, "He just wants me to be happy."

"I'm sure he does."

Gretchen bit her tongue against warning Joanie again about Tony's temper. She hoped it was something that he was getting help for. It wasn't her place at all to be a part of that.

FOR EASTER BREAK, Gretchen took the girls down to Palo Alto to see her folks. Kate and little Grady joined them, coming up from Coronado, since Tyler was also on deployment with Trace. Mr. and Mrs. Morgan took them to the Junior Museum and attended a Saturday play at a local children's theater.

Grady was trying to crawl on a coverlet spread out for him as they sat in the backyard. Rebecca and Angie loved giving him colorful blocks and then taking them away, trying to encourage him to reach and crawl to get the prize.

"You and Trace still close?" Kate asked.

"I think so. But things are on ice a bit, with the deployment."

"He'll call you eventually. They have to be careful."

"Do you know where they are?" Gretchen asked.

Kate shrugged. "Sort of. Christy kind of spilled the beans. I don't know where exactly, but it's in the Caribbean. And you cannot tell a soul I told you."

"No worries. But, actually, that makes me feel better. I was worried it was Africa or the Middle East."

"My sentiments exactly. The only thing dangerous about the Caribbean are the pretty girls in the skimpy bikinis and the rum."

The two sisters laughed.

"I was going to go over to the cemetery tomorrow to visit—" Gretchen stumbled on the word.

"Your father's grave. I think you should. Will you take Clover?"

"Not yet. Not time yet for that."

"You want some company?" Kate asked.

"Do you think Dad would mind?"

"Not a chance. He'd probably drive you over if you asked him."

Gretchen had recently found out that the man who raised her, and whom she considered her father, was not her biological dad. Her mother had fallen in love with a young Marine on an airplane trip to Portland, as it happened, while she had a boyfriend in California she was breaking up with. One thing led to another, and her mother became pregnant. The Marine was killed on his next deployment in Southeast Asia. But before he died, he had written some of the most beautiful letters Gretchen had ever seen.

When their mom met their dad, he accepted Gretchen as his own.

THE MORGANS TOOK the girls shopping while Kate and Gretchen went to the Veterans Cemetery nearby. She'd visited his grave many times before and often wondered what he was like.

She knelt by the headstone and brushed pine needles off the cool surface of the white granite. Rows of American flags blew in the breeze, sounding like sails on little boats out on the bay. Kate stood behind her.

"I should have brought some flowers."

"No, Gretchen. He knows what's in your heart. I'll bet he's smiling down on you right now."

She closed her eyes and decided to talk to him.

Dad, if you are there, I just wanted to say that although I never met you in person, through your letters I've come to understand and love who you are and how you loved my mother. Thank you for that. Thank you for writing those beautiful letters so I could get even a glimpse of who you are.

I supposed you know Mom is very happy, and the man I call Dad has been a real father to me in every way except one.

I have a favor to ask of you. I met someone very special to me, and he's serving with Kate's husband, Tyler, on a mission of some kind. Watch over them both. Bring them both back safely. I know you'll be their guardian. But don't go appear to them and scare the liver out of them!

Love you, Dad. I always will. Until I see you some day.

CHAPTER 22

TRACE AND THE rest of their squad were briefed in the old chapel at the base camp they'd called "Sparrow Lodge" after the mythical pirate. They'd spent nearly a week clearing jungle foliage and debris blown over from the recent hurricanes. The island had taken a direct hit, and power hadn't been restored to some of the remote parts until recently. The international team of health workers was still finding bodies of dead animals and missing humans.

That didn't stop the resilient people from making merry, and everywhere work crews were painting new signs or sidewalls of shops and houses with their characteristic bright turquoise and hot pink colors so prevalent on the island.

The campsite had been abandoned when it was determined it would take more than the property was worth for the church to restore it, even though the chapel was nearly three hundred years old. Uncle Sam made some brownie points with the Archdiocese and, at the same time, garnered one of the highest peaks on the island with a view of the blue Caribbean Sea from any direction. A tracking station would be installed, and it even had an old concrete landing strip created back in the forties when a variety of underworld figures populated the island. With enough manpower, it could be fortified just like a real fort. Two military transport Jeeps were abandoned, and Coop got them running in no time. Luckily, the stored gas cans were uncontaminated and could be used.

The stones used to create the chapel were embedded with shells and fossils of sea creatures from eons ago. It was porous and chalky, so it also housed varieties of geckos, as well as mossy lichen that would squeeze through the tiny cracks in the stone. The damp, musty smell was more like the hull of an old sailing ship than a church. Part of the roof had been blown off, which allowed a family of birds to nest in the large wooden cross well-fastened above the baptistery.

"One of our first building projects, now that the clearings have been created, is to fix this roof. In the coming months, the rainfall will begin, and it will make this building uninhabitable," Kyle said.

He had opened up a metal tripod, which contained some enlarged photographs on poster paper, all clipped at the top to hold them in place.

"We're here to find this man." Kyle pointed to a picture of a dark-faced man with a grin that seemed to extend from ear to ear. His gold teeth on his upper jaw were embedded with dollar signs and pairs of dice. Trace had thought, at first, he had bugs on his teeth until he'd looked closer. His teeth were stained red from chewing local fruits with the bright red seeds like pomegranate. He wore a top hat made of bright red satin, patched and woven with feathers, shells, and sticks painted various colors.

"This is King Henry. He likes to tell people he runs the island. And if he doesn't run some portion of the island, then it's not worth it," Kyle said.

"This,"—Kyle flipped the poster over, revealing a medium-sized cruise ship painted with huge murals of sea horses and rainbows—patterns more befitting a child's nursery than a ship in the middle of the ocean—"is where he lives. His ship, the Queen Amalie, was sunk at sea in a terrorist attack off the coast of West Africa. He brought it to port some ten years ago and has completely remodeled this ship, adding a communications tower and helipad."

Distinctively, it flew the flag of St. Croix, but it also flew a bright red and black pirate's flag, the skull and crossbones twice the size of the other one. On the skull's head was a crown, worn cocked at an angle screaming defiance.

"Right now, King Henry has the run of the British as well as the US Virgin Islands. His tentacles are deep. He's got a network of agents who work on all the islands in the Caribbean. The Queen Amalie travels between Florida, Puerto Rico, South America, and Cuba, buying and selling wares. He has eluded raids and capture. He berths most frequently on St. Croix, so part of our mission here is to track his comings and goings. He rarely is seen on land. We think he traffics in drugs and recently has expanded into the human slave trade."

The team shifted, stretching their legs on the uncomfortable stone benches. Kyle's voice echoed off the barren walls.

Trace hadn't had a good night's sleep since they arrived. The jungle night sounds woke him up constantly, and the blowup mattress sprung a leak that he was still trying to figure out how to fix. If they made it to town soon, he'd just buy a couple of thick comforters, if he could find them cheap enough, and use those until the jungle moisture saturated them.

The jungle won out over everything.

The old stone structures looked like barracks at one time, room enough for a group of five or six. Windows would have to come later. For now, nothing was air or water tight. They all had to get used to the wet jungle breeze covering everything by morning.

His phone reception was non-existent, since so many of the cell towers had to be rebuilt after the two hurricanes. He would have to wait until they went into town before he'd be able to get through to Gretchen.

At night, they made a bonfire. So much foliage and debris had been removed and piled up they had more than enough to burn for their entire stay. It became a nightly tradition. Kyle and the others, who had worked missions in Mexico, spoke about the drug trade. Since Trace's SEAL Team in Little Creek was mainly tasked with the African theater, they rarely saw any action in Mexico or South America. He listened and learned.

The next day, nine in their squad ventured into the town of Frederiksted, where all the larger ships docked. They'd been told King Henry might make an appearance at midnight.

Kyle asked them to split up into groups of no less than four and to wander the streets, looking for bars and restaurants that would make good meeting places. They were to listen for any talk of King Henry and any pictures or evidence that he frequented the town or had friends there.

Trace found a vendor who sold blankets and bedspreads, so he could supplement the flattened air mattress. He carried the large parcel around with him all afternoon. It was hot and sticky, but well worth the price for a good night's sleep. Everywhere he went, people stared at him.

Nearing midnight, Trace spread the blankets on the beach, and they sat, drinking local beer and dining on jerk chicken and hot "mystery" sausages. The Queen Amalie arrived about a half hour later, pulling quietly, with its lights dimmed, up to the pier that had earlier been occupied by a Scandinavian cruise ship. The sounds of music and heavy partying echoed off the water and against the boarded up village of vendors and stores just past the pier.

Light was scarce, but Trace followed the shadows back and forth with night vision binoculars. He saw partygoers entering and exiting the ship in various stages of drunkenness. Small groups of men and women or couples—all well-dressed guests—passed by a line of crew members dressed in white. A police car drove halfway down the pier, its blue lights flashing, which blocked out the effectiveness of the scopes. It stopped next to the gangway, and he could barely make out two people in the vehicle, but neither of them got out.

"We should get a closer look," Trace said.

"Let me check this out," said Coop, taking the goggles. "Hey, Lannie, I think King Henry just stepped off the ship and got in the police cruiser."

"No shit?" Kyle used his scope to verify. "I'm not

seeing it. You sure?"

"He's got everything but the hat. I'd bet all of my allowance on it."

Coop passed around the NVG. Several others confirmed what Coop had seen. Trace repeated his request. "We gotta get down there to get closer."

"Fredo, you brought the camera, I hope?"

"Yup, boss. If we could get them to turn off those damned lights, we could get some real clear pictures you could upload. I think Trace is right. Just send a couple of us."

"Alright. Fredo, you give the camera over to Danny, if you don't mind. Trace, you, T.J., and Danny go down there. See what you can shoot."

"I got you covered, boys," Armando said, pulling out his Desert Tech SRS–A1 recon scout rifle and snapping his scope in place. "You show me the sign, and I'll lighten the crowd size."

"Just don't get caught, that's all," added Kyle. We need a couple of pix, and then you're back here in five, ten at the most, you hear?"

"Copy that."

All three of them inserted their Invisios and did a sound check. Fredo gave a thumbs up, and the three took off down the beach. A metal culvert bisected their approach, but gave good cover. Trace checked the upper pier for snipers or spotters. Danny did the same.

"I think we're okay," T.J. said. "We want to come up that ladder to the dock. It's so dark I don't think anyone will see us. But you see the flare of a flashlight, we flatten, okay?"

"Roger that," Trace said. "Why did I have to open my big mouth?"

Danny grinned and slapped his back silently, whispering, "Because you're the new guy, that's why. New guys go first. Didn't they teach you that in Little Creek?"

"Hey, they told me the West Coast guys never saw much action. I thought I was going back to kindergarten."

"Fuck you, Bennett," Kyle whispered, listening to their chatter. "Just get your butts on that pier and do your thing. This ain't no coffee break."

They ran in a crouching gait until they hit the concrete piles. Danny scrambled up the ladder without making a sound. T.J. went next.

When Trace reached the top of the decking, Danny and T.J. were kneeling behind a row of oil drums. The flashing lights on the police vehicle made it impossible to use their night gear. For mere seconds at a time, they had a distorted view of the guarded gangway, the line of revelers, and activity on board the ship. Cabin lights randomly dotted the profile of the ship. Sounds of music got louder and then faded as doors to the interior were opened and then closed. Trace thought there could be hundreds on board, plus the crew.

With the sound of Danny's camera recording the scene, the back door of the blue and white police cruiser opened and someone slid into the seat. Danny positioned his camera and got a couple shots. In the strobe, a face was illuminated. There was no mistaking it.

King Henry and a woman in a dancer's costume sat side by side. He lit a cigarette for them both and handed her one. The glow on the lighter confirmed what they'd seen.

"You get that?" T.J. asked as the car sped off without a siren.

"Sure thing. So he gets a police escort. Wish we had something to follow him."

Trace was thinking he'd love to get on board that ship and do some playing around. "Kyle, can we attempt to board? With our target on land, they're not going anywhere."

"Not tonight, Trace, but thanks for volunteering. Let's get this info uploaded and call it a night."

Danny was the first one over the edge, followed by T.J. Trace slipped his binoculars back into his front pocket. The Velcro opening made too much noise, and in the next instant, he froze.

One of the security detail had him nailed with a

flashlight. Two other guards came up alongside them and began running in his direction, guns drawn.

"Stop!"

"Fuck," Trace muttered.

"Give me the sign," answered Armando.

"Hold it, Armani. Not yet." Trace heard the tension in Kyle's voice. But he knew it was the smart play not to go firing off rounds and causing a scene.

"They're asking me to stand," whispered Trace.

"You dumb sonofabitch. You got your wish. Now let's see how you manage to get out of this one. Be cool, and for fuck's sake, don't lose your Invisio." Kyle followed up his command with a string of swear words.

Trace stood, as he was told. He didn't have anything but his dog tags and a wallet with little cash. He was grateful he didn't have a firearm, but it made him feel naked.

It wasn't the kind of naked he'd been looking forward to.

CHAPTER 23

GRETCHEN WAS SERVED with papers just as she was getting ready to take the girls to school. The young process server with a knit cap had been waiting in the bushes, and as she loaded up the car and double-checked Angie's seatbelt, he approached her from behind and scared her to death.

He ran down the long steep driveway and onto the street below, picking up a skateboard as his escape vehicle.

Gretchen wanted to look at the papers, but didn't dare do so. She handed the bundle to Clover, sitting next to her.

"Put these in the glove box, please."

"What is that?" asked Angie.

"A love letter from your father," Gretchen spouted off. Then she apologized and corrected herself. "It's something your dad and I are working out."

Clover gave her a long, sad look and then turned to

face the windshield. Her heavy blinking indicated she'd started to tear up.

Gretchen started the car, leaned over, and placed her hand on Clover's sleeve. "Don't worry. It's all going to be okay. I promise."

Clover didn't return her gaze. She was stoic, her face slightly more pale than usual.

Hang in there, Clover. I've got the butterflies, too.

After dropping Clover and Rebecca at school, she took Angela to the church preschool, which started nearly an hour later. She was hoping they'd take her early.

"Sweetheart, Mommy's got to make a phone call, so I'm going to drop you off early if someone's there, okay?"

"No problem," her meek little voice answered. Gretchen noted that even Angie was scared.

The school director's car was in the parking lot, so Gretchen took Angie by the hand and entered through the back door. The church hallway was dark except for the warm, yellow light coming from the director's office.

Though the door was ajar, she knocked anyway, holding Angela's hand firmly.

"Connie?"

"Hi, Gretchen. You're here very early."

"Yeah, I know. Listen, I just got some bad news,

and I need to take care of a couple things. Is it okay if I leave Angie here early?"

Connie smiled and held out her arms. "Of course you can leave this little munchkin here." Angela ran to her arms and returned the hug.

"Thanks. I owe you, big time."

"Well, I've got some paper and colored pens she can use while I get some planning done. You won't be late to pickup, will you?"

"No, I'm going to have Carole come get her, or one of the other carpool moms, if I can. But either way, she'll be picked up on time. Thanks a bunch."

She kissed Angie and jogged to the car.

A shadow came from the bushes at the side of the old church and, before she reached the door handle, cut off her access.

It was Tony.

His hair was disheveled with several-day-old stubble on his chin, and his eyes were bloodshot. She could smell alcohol on his breath.

She took several steps backward until she stepped over a parking barrier and nearly tripped. Tony grabbed her by the coat lapel and pulled her toward him. His breath was foul.

"Let me go!" she said as she struggled.

"So you thought you'd be so smart, did you? Got your papers? See what happens when you try to fight me?"

"What are you saying?" She threw his arms to the side and off her coat.

"You little goodie two shoes. Miss perfect. You just thought you could take those girls away from me, didn't you?"

"I've done no such thing. Tony, you're drunk. You need to get hold of yourself, or I'll call the police."

"Right. And they'll get great tickets to the next home game for their troubles. You can't use me like that."

"I have no idea what you're talking about. I haven't done anything like that."

"Then why won't you let them come live with me? You think my money isn't as good as yours, huh? Or is it Joanie? You're jealous."

"Hardly. If she wants you, she can certainly have you. That's not on my mind, Tony."

His eyes glazed over for a couple of seconds, and Gretchen wondered if he was having a stroke. But he righted himself and seemed to not know where he was.

"Tony, you need to see a doctor."

He laughed bitterly. "I already did. And I'm suspended for five days."

"Sorry to hear that. Maybe you should go home, take care of yourself, and get some rest. I'm guessing that's why they did it."

She'd heard some talk on one of the sports recaps that Tony's game had faltered recently. But she'd brushed it off as idle gossip.

Her ex grabbed her by the coat again and kissed her hard on the mouth. The sudden movement confused her. She twisted her head to the side and tried to fend off his determined kiss, but he was too strong for her. His left hand went inside her coat, feeling up her blouse while his other arm held her securely in place. His eyes were half-lidded and filled with lust.

"You remember I fucked you good. I was the best fuck of your life."

Continuing to struggle, she tried to stomp on his foot and then kneed him in the groin. He doubled over in pain.

"You are an animal. Stay away from me."

She got inside the car and locked it, turned on the ignition, and drove down the street. Checking her rearview mirror, she didn't see that he followed her.

Her mind reeled from the encounter. She had to contact her mother, perhaps Tyler's mother as well. And she had to contact the attorney and tell him about the papers.

Tears streamed down her face, and she felt her insides collapse. Tony had always been a butthead, a royal pain that she put up with because of the girls. But now he was scaring her. She recalled Joanie's bruise and decided her first order of business was to report this encounter to the police. Something was very wrong.

"I want to report an assault," she said to the woman behind the thick window at the police station.

The uniformed clerk pushed a clipboard with paperwork under the glass barrier. "Please fill this out and sign it. I'll ask someone to come out and take your statement."

Gretchen took the clipboard and looked it over.

"When did this happen?" the clerk asked. "You look a little upset. Did you just come from where this encounter?"

"Yes, I dropped my daughter off at preschool, and he came after me. He must have been waiting for me to show up."

"Okay, well, you sit down, and I'll have someone come out there right away. Are you injured in any way?"

"No, ma'am."

"Is this person known to you?"

"Yes, he's my ex-husband."

"Has he ever done this before?"

"Not since the divorce. But then, that's partially why we divorced."

"Why don't you have a seat, ma'am? Just finish the paperwork, and I'll get an officer to come out."

The writing on the incident report was so small it was difficult to see. Her hands shook, and then she discovered her tears obscured the letters. Already several drops had fallen on the form, blurring her writing. She took several deep breaths and finished.

Slipping the clipboard under the Plexiglas barrier, she was asked to sit down again. Her mind reeled from everything that had happened today. She still hadn't read over the summons, and she needed to call her mom.

Then she thought about Connie all alone at the preschool, and panic set in. She dialed the director's cell number and didn't get an answer.

She flew to the window, banging on the glass. "Please, please. I need to talk to someone right now!"

The clerk returned. "It will be just a few more minutes."

"No, you don't understand. He might be at my daughter's school. He might try to kidnap her!"

The clerk said something in her shoulder microphone. A door at the side buzzed and opened wide enough to allow a uniformed officer to show himself. He asked her to come inside, and she was taken to an interview room.

"I don't have your paperwork, but why don't you calm down and tell me what this is all about?"

The clerk passed him the clipboard with Gretchen's

information about the incident.

He did have kind eyes, but they were unfamiliar. It stressed her out that she had to convince him she wasn't crazy or imagining things.

"My ex-husband served me with what I think is custody papers this morning. I dropped my daughter off at her preschool, and he was waiting there, came running out from the bushes. It scared me to death. He was drunk, not like himself. And now I'm wondering if he went inside the school. I'm worried for my daughter. I need to check on her."

The officer put wheels in motion quickly. "I'll take you as soon as I get my partner. Be right back.

He closed the door behind him, and Gretchen wanted to bolt. Too much time had passed by.

The officer returned with his female partner, and the three of them left the station, Gretchen in the back seat of the police cruiser. She gave them directions, and while on the way, his partner asked her about her ex, wondering if this was chronic or a habit.

Gretchen told her about the bruises on Joanie's neck.

When they arrived at the church, Gretchen ran from the car, through the rear door, and down the hallway. This time, children were hanging up coats and pairs of parents stood by or hugged their children good-bye. The police were not far behind. The group of parents and children clustered in groups, and the hallway started buzzing with concern and whispers.

When Gretchen got to the door of the director's office, it was vacant.

"She's gone! The director's gone. My daughter isn't here!"

"Excuse me. Officers, can I help you?" Connie's voice boomed from the end of the hallway near one of the classrooms.

"Ma'am, we've had a complaint of a harassing father—" She looked to her partner, who stepped forward.

"We've been told to come check on this woman's daughter. She's afraid she is in danger."

Gretchen passed him by on her way to the director. "Connie, Tony assaulted me in the parking lot. Is Angie here? He didn't take her, did he?"

The woman hesitated at first then eyed both the police officers. "She's fine. She's right here, if you need to see her." She motioned to the classroom. Her expression showed worry and confusion. "Angie, Mommy's here."

"Goody!" she heard her daughter say before she came running and hugged her legs. "Are you going to go to school with me today?"

Gretchen broke down in tears. She'd made a complete fool of herself. Kneeling down, she hugged

Angela, sobbing.

"What's wrong?" Angie asked.

"Mommy's fine. I just got worried, that's all." She released her daughter and then spoke to the director. "Did Tony come by after I left?"

She shook her head. "Nope. I haven't seen Tony in several weeks."

Gretchen knew all the way back to the station that she'd overreacted, but she justified it because of her fear for her daughter's safety. But even she had to admit to the officers that Tony, while he'd shown increasing anger toward her, had never shown it to the kids.

Her apologies were accepted. They recommended she get some help figuring out all the legal issues she would now be facing, and when she asked them about the assault charges, she was given another longer form, asked to go home and fill it out, and drop it off to the station or mail it in.

Armed with her collection of brochures on child abuse, divorce with children, and spousal abuse, as well as the adult version Incident Report, she returned to her car, sat down, put her head on the steering wheel over her hands, and cried.

CHAPTER 24

THE BEAUTY OF the Invisios the Team used was that they were so small, no one could tell they were being worn. Trace had put his so far inside his ear canal he was beginning to wonder if he'd be able to get it out afterwards. That happened occasionally to guys. The little microphone worked off the bone structures in the inner ear, so the quality of the sound was nearly as good as the quality of hearing the owner had.

This meant just about everything going on around him, being said to him face-to-face, could be picked up by the Team, unless he were more than a thousand yards away. He wasn't quite sure if the metal hull of the ship would block a signal, but guessed it would interfere. So he whispered, as if talking to himself, making like he was drunk and perhaps a bit crazy, which might lessen the guard's attention. He had no idea what he was going to tell them.

The guards nudged him over to the tiny terminal

about the size of an outhouse at the end of the gangway. He was frisked and cuffed, chained to a metal awning pole.

"So, mon, you no can go here without permission." He held up Trace's wallet and pulled out all his cash, a whopping forty US. "Dis," he said as he waved the cash in the air, "is not permission." The dark-skinned man was missing every other tooth. His face was leathery and wrinkled like a prune. His eyes looked mean and extremely nasty.

"I apologize," Trace started to say.

"Where you from?"

"C-California. Look, fellas, I don't want any trouble."

"Oh, mon, trouble is what you got big time."

One of the other guards, who fit the description of a muffin top if there ever was one, chuckled, his belly rippling over his belt. He chewed on a toothpick calmly while Trace squirmed.

It wasn't hard to act scared. He'd fucked up and gotten himself caught.

"What's a California man doing here on God's Island?"

"I was drinking last night downtown—"

"What town is that?" The guard turned to his two buddies. "You know a place called *downtown*?"

They both shrugged, and Mr. Pruneface aimed his

beady eyes back on Trace.

"Fredricksburg or something like that."

"Ah, he was in Fred's town. *Dat* town."

The other two guards nodded wisely and said, "Ah," in unison.

Trace waited for further instructions. Finally, the guard poked him with his forefinger. "Talk. You were drinking, and—?"

"I overheard a conversation about this ship, the Emily, or Amily or something. They told me it would be coming in at midnight. Said it was tons of fun."

"Except it's for club members only, Mr. California. You got to pay the dues first. Not for free."

"Well, that's why I climbed the pier. I was hoping to bypass that ticket taker down there. Thought my forty bucks would get me in."

"No, my man. Your forty bucks makes sure you stay out. You go to jail, mon. This is breaking and entering. Ever heard of dat?"

Trace knew he was just messing with him.

"I get paid on Friday. I'll have more cash then. Can I get a temporary loan?"

That brought down the house in raucous laughter. He saw passengers on board turn and look in his direction.

"Dis guy. Dis guy is a funny man. What do you do, Mr. California?"

"I'm in the Navy. I'm a Seabee."

"A what?"

"A Seabee. We build things for the Navy. Like a contractor."

"And what are you building on our God's island?"

"It's a campground."

"Nobody goes camping on our island. This isn't California."

"I realize that. It's a US government facility. We're building toilets and little cabins, restoring the old church."

"Sounds like the Peace Corps. You in the Peace Corps, Mr. California?"

"No, sir, I told you. I'm employed by the Navy."

The head guard considered his options. Trace thought perhaps he could confuse him a bit before he made up his mind. Either way it went, whatever he would decide wouldn't be good for Trace, so he tried to take a little control.

"Look, man. I'll come back tomorrow night. I'll even bring some buddies. How's that? And we'll bring more money this time. We're just here to have a good time. Meet some girls. You know, get a little, you know. We're not here to hurt anyone. But if I wind up missing, the Navy will come looking for me."

"You wouldn't be the first sailor who got lost on our island. What you don't want is to get yourself disappeared."

The guard walked around Trace, studying his clothes, his shoes, looking for a watch or ring, something obviously worth something he could steal. Trace's bladder almost gave out when the guard examined his earlobes for evidence of an earring. He missed the Invisio.

"Well, I'm afraid, son, you've got bad luck, and we don't let anyone on the ship with bad luck. We are leaving before the sun comes up and headed to another island. So I'm afraid your buddies won't be able to visit this place. But we'll be back. How long will you be here?"

"I think several months. Until the job is finished, I imagine."

"Well then, it's a date. You come back in about thirty days. We'll be right here. We always arrive at the witching hour, midnight!" he said with his eyes wide and his hands splayed over his head. "You remember old Jonny here, okay?"

"Sure. Sure. I promise."

"And just for your information, it will be two hundred US per person. That's the ticket price."

"Just for one evening?"

"No, sir. We take you someplace else, and we drop you. You have to find the way home! That's the way it works." All three of the guards cackled.

Trace looked up at the ship, so close and yet so far away. But he remembered what their mission was. It wasn't the ship. It was King George. He smiled back to the guard as the handcuffs were removed.

"Thirty days, it is. Does anyone have the schedule? We have to ask permission to leave ahead of time. Any idea what date?"

The guard squinted briefly. Trace wondered if he'd overplayed his hand.

"The pink mermaid bar in Fred's town always knows. You can inquire there and tell Ida you're a friend of Jonny's. I'm always on guard when the ship comes in for the King. You know the King?"

"No, I don't. I heard that some rich guy owns this. He's a king?"

"He is da king of our island. You got a king in Washington, D.C. Next time, I'll introduce you. Be prepared to pay. Nothing is free."

Trace decided Jonny had become an ally. So he asked a burning question, "How many times have you sailed on her?"

"Queen Amalie? That bitch is a hard one. Never."

Jonny even shook Trace's hand. When he started to climb over the pier, the guard stopped him.

"No, no! Not that way. You walk out like a guest. Dat way." He pointed down the long pier, which meant it would take him at least thirty minutes before he could meet up with the rest of the Team.

"Trace, you're a fuckin' genius," Kyle said in his

ear.

"Well, I was hoping for a look inside that ship. Next time."

"Because of you, there will be a next time, and you got a personal invitation to meet the King himself. I'd say job well done."

THE PHOTOS AND intel was transmitted. The Headshed were thrilled with what they'd obtained. A combined expedition would be set up after several of the SEALs had been on board to scope out the environment. Kyle told the group that SEAL Team 3 would be leading a boarding party next deployment after the task force was created. Until then, their job had been deemed complete one hundred percent.

"Best news is, we get to go home early, gents. Thanks to the new guy, Frogman Trace Bennett."

He was toasted several times over the next two days as they prepared to store and lock up equipment and supplies they'd brought. They took inventory of what to bring next time. An advance team would set up the clearance, and then they'd drop in at night when the port remained empty.

Trace could hardly wait to get to talk to Gretchen again. Whether it was California or Portland, he was going home.

CHAPTER 25

GRETCHEN MET WITH the attorney when she was visiting her mother in Palo Alto, who, after listening to the issues involved, put her in touch with a Portland child custody attorney. The office visit was gratis, but she'd have to pay for the visit in Portland.

The encounter with Tony had left her shaken. Her mother encouraged her to move out of the house and to come down and stay with her indefinitely, until things ironed out. As strange as Tony's behavior was, Gretchen didn't think he'd do anything stupid, really stupid. Her mother cautioned her about being overly confident.

"I just worry so much about you and the girls. I mean, your dad and I are so far away. We couldn't get there in time if something were to happen. Should we come up there?"

"No, Mom. I think you should stay out of it."

"But what about the girls? Wouldn't they feel safer

if we came?"

Gretchen considered it and promised she'd call her back after the interview with the new attorney.

Delmar Bernstein's office was on the top floor of one of the tallest buildings in downtown Portland. The commanding view of the Columbia River and across into Washington State was breathtaking, especially on a day like today. Huge billowy clouds swept across the bright blue sky. Some had grey patches at the edges, and rain dumped down on the city below. It truly felt like you were God sitting on top, watching the minions below. Sheets of silvery water fell at all angles, and sunlight illuminated the landscape, increasing the sparkle with puddles and washes of streets and sidewalks.

Mr. Bernstein didn't react to her comment about his lovely office. He was focused on her case, which made her feel better.

"I'm going to tell you a couple of things first. I've talked to your mother's friend, and he also gave me some additional information. There was an incident with your ex-husband a couple of days ago?"

"Yes, at Angie's school."

"Unfortunately, the police report is not going to do us any favors. Mr. Sanders's attorney has already spoken to them, and they've also interviewed the preschool director. They're playing for keeps. I know

Ms. Hainstock, and she's a worthy opponent, so we need to establish some ground rules."

"Fine." Gretchen's calm demeanor evaporated.

"First, you're not to have any communication with Mr. Sanders. I'm going to move that he have no visitation until after the settlement, especially because of his actions. We might not get that granted, but I don't want anything that could negatively reflect on you to occur, or we'll leave a door the size of the White House they can drive their trucks through and take the kids. Understood?"

"Y-Yes."

"You know your ex-husband has considerable assets. I'm prepared to say he's going to throw a lot of money at this. He's not the party who should win, but by investigating things so thoroughly, they could tie you up for months and drag anything from your past up and make it look like you're a bag lady or something. So be forewarned."

"I understand. But I thought women, the mother in these cases, usually has a stronger side."

"Stronger? Perhaps. But if they challenge everything about you and don't stop, you're going to run out of money. Gretchen..." He leaned forward, his palms on his spotless blotter. "I don't work for free."

"I get it. I'll get you paid."

"If it comes to that, I can perhaps do some work

pro bono or get you referred out. But this is child custody, not a murder trial. He with the most bucks usually wins, I'm sorry to say."

Gretchen gulped down air. Her hands were sweaty. She felt her underarms hot and dripping with perspiration. The coffee she'd had on the way over burned a hole in her stomach. In a few minutes, she'd have to run to the bathroom. The whole world had tuned on itself, and she suddenly felt victimized, yanked from her safe perch in the house she loved with the most important people around her. Lazy afternoons wandering through museums and book stores with the girls now seemed such a luxury. She'd not prepared for this.

She could not lose this fight. If she did, it would kill her.

Mr. Bernstein smiled. "Now for the good part. From what I can tell, you're a perfect mom. One can forgive your little incident the other day. You'd just been served papers, something out of the blue. You were busy just being a mom and concentrating on doing that. Then Mr. Sanders shows up. And of course you worry because Clover has just been kidnapped not two weeks before. I get it. We have to make sure the judge gets it, too. In your shoes, my wife would have probably done the same."

Gretchen thought of something else. "What about the bruises on Joanie's neck? And the fact that Clover was abducted under their watch?"

"We have to be careful not to make an enemy of her. If she was in fact abused, you need her as an ally. I know that sucks, having to be friends with your ex's fiancée, but try to be pleasant to her. Don't engage, and certainly don't do anything to upset her."

"Oh, we get along fine. She's like me. Well, not exactly like me, but she's in the stage where she doesn't believe Tony's the monster I know him to be."

"And we have another piece of good news. Apparently, Mr. Sanders is being considered for a trade. So perhaps that's what's driving all this custody battle. He might have to move clear across the country. That would mean he wouldn't get to see the girls as much. They'll probably try for some joint decision where Mr. Sanders pays for all the travel costs. It will be something that will be hard to fight, since he clearly can afford that arrangement. We don't want to look like the jilted or jealous ex-wife."

"I see your point. So all the more important to remain on good terms with Joanie. But you say not to reach out to her at all."

"Absolutely not. At this point, whose side will she come down on? Yours or his?"

"I understand. What about the team doctor? Can he be forced to give a statement? I know something is going on with Tony. Drinking more. I never recall him being suspended before. This is all new behavior."

"We can't go there. Mr. Sanders is an asset to the team. Anything they do that diminishes that asset's value would be pure folly. They want to trade him probably because of his behavior, but you won't get them to say it on the record."

The rest of the conversation involved the procedure, what he was going to work on next. He asked a lot of questions about Tony's habits and public displays of "naughty boy syndrome," as he called it. And, sadly, he said it was not uncommon that the players who made such enormous salaries began to believe their own press until they couldn't deliver to the hype. To an elite athlete, going beyond one's prime was a hard fact of life. He told Gretchen often everyone around the celebrity was blamed for something that was just caused by Mother Nature or enhanced by some substance abuse, which magnifies it.

At the end of their hour-long appointment, she wrote Bernstein a check with funds her mother loaned to her. Her mom'd tried to give it to Gretchen, but she insisted on taking it as a loan. And she asked him about having her mother and father come stay with her for a few days or weeks.

"I'd do it. Gretchen, you're going to need every ounce of help you can get. And don't you have a boyfriend who is a Navy SEAL? We gotta make sure he's at one of these hearings, you know, wearing his dress whites?"

"We're just good friends. My brother-in-law serves on the same SEAL Team. I'm sure Tyler would help out, even if Trace isn't available. We're not to the stage where I can call him my boyfriend."

Bernstein smiled and nodded. "I see. Well, if you want my advice, *make* him your boyfriend. I don't think there's a more honorable group of men on the planet than those SEALs. We all owe them a lot."

Gretchen's eyes teared up, and she brushed them away with the back of her hands. The timing of everything just sucked. She was overwhelmed. She knew Tony would slowly bleed her and her whole family dry if she let him. Full of second guesses, she had a hard time feeling brave.

"You've done a great job with the girls."

"That's what everyone says. But it doesn't mean I won't lose them. All because I don't have enough money."

"Unfortunately, that's the way of things. But, sometimes, a miracle happens, and it turns out the way it's supposed to. In theory, no matter how much money you have, the right person should win. Let's hope for a little luck, pray Tony continues his bad behavior without hurting anyone, and get your family firmly packed around you so you don't spend a minute doubting yourself. But prepare yourself, kid. It's going to be brutal."

Gretchen walked to her car, letting the rain fall on her face and hair. The coolness of the water was calming. She knew she was strong. She just wasn't sure how hard she could fight if she was this wounded. Taking the girls away from her would be something she could never recover from.

Would life be worth living?

That scared her most of all.

CHAPTER 26

THE TEAM TOUCHED American soil in Virginia and then took a double stopover flight, landing them in San Diego at midnight. Trace had left one message for Gretchen telling her he was on his way home. He texted her that he was back in San Diego.

Tyler jogged over before Trace took off from the Team building. His bags were stowed, and he was anxious for a hot shower and a good night's sleep.

"Has Gretchen gotten hold of you?"

Trace's stomach dropped. "No. What's going on?"

"I guess there's been some kind of incident with Tony. Kate's mom and dad have flown up to be with her and the girls. Tony filed some legal papers, custody papers or some shit. She's had to get an attorney. She's filed a police report. Sounds like things are coming unraveled."

"Holy shit. I just tried to text her. Is she okay? Did that sonofabitch hurt her?"

"Not that I know of, Trace." Tyler dropped his hands and swore. "Argh! I shouldn't have told you. Now I've managed to get you upset, too. Sorry, Trace."

"No. No. I want to know. I just can't reach her right now. Do you have her mother's or dad's number?"

"I'll have to call Kate. But she's up with the baby. I'm sure she wouldn't mind."

Before Tyler got the alternate number, Gretchen called.

"I just heard. Are you okay?"

"Yes, we're all fine. Oh man, I don't know where to begin. My folks came up, and I'm so grateful."

"Tell me what you can. I should come up there, too."

"I can't ask you to do that."

"You didn't ask. I'm offering. I'll have to check in with Kyle first, but if you think I'd be of assistance, I'm there."

"Well, Tony's filed for custody of the girls, and he has a really expensive and apparently good attorney. That's a big thing, but the biggest thing is… Trace, I'm afraid of him. He surprised me when I dropped Angie off at preschool, just pounced from the bushes, his hands grabbing me everywhere—"

"Fuckin' sonofabitch. You told the cops, right?"

"Yes, I filed the report—oh, I didn't behave well that day, so I'm sure they think I'm a basket case. But I was so preoccupied with the papers. I overreacted a bit. My attorney is going to court tomorrow to bar him from coming by the house to see the girls or be anywhere near me."

"That sounds like a good plan." Trace's impatience was making him think fuzzy. "I'd feel a whole lot better if I got there. It just wouldn't be right if something happened and I could have prevented it."

"I know the action tomorrow morning won't go over very well with Tony. Especially if he loses. If you can, I'd love it. And the girls have been asking about you, too."

"Done. I'll text you when I arrive. Can your dad or someone pick me up at the airport?"

"Of course."

"So what did he do? Did he try something...*funny*?"

"He was a wild man. Kissed me, tried to fondle me. He doesn't care anything about me. It's just that he's losing everything."

"A man like that can be dangerous. Please be careful. Fingers crossed here. Let me see if I can locate Kyle, and I'll text you my ETA." He sighed, settling his nerves. Now that he had another mission planned, he was much calmer.

It was, after all, what he was made for.

TRACE GOT PERMISSION to travel to Portland and caught the first flight out, landing mid-morning. Joe Morgan met him at the airport. The older man stepped right out of the crowd and called his name. They shook hands.

"Glad you figured it out. Don't know what I'd have done, Joe, if you hadn't. I'd be wandering the airport instead of lending assistance."

"Kate showed me pictures of your trip to Hawaii. There's a nice one of you and Gretchen," he said as he raised the trunk so Trace could load up his bag. "Never seen her so happy before," he said over the top of the car as they each got in to their sides.

"How's she holding up?"

"She's scared, I won't lie. Clover was telling me his eyes looked funny and he smelled bad. Gretchen says he's been on a bender for a few days. You know he actually caused his fiancée some bruising on her neck?"

"No shit?" Trace covered his mouth. "Sorry, sir."

"Oh, shoot. We're so used to Tyler and the things he can spew out, that was tame. Louise says I'm starting to pick up the SEAL lingo. Can you imagine that, learning to swear at sixty-eight years of age?"

Trace liked the man instantly. "Well, they say that which doesn't destroy you makes you stronger. We swear a lot so we don't cry. We can get awfully serious on some of these missions. It takes the edge off and helps us think straight if we relax a bit. Know what I mean?"

"I know exactly what you mean, son."

Trace thought about the story Gretchen had told him about Joe not being her biological father. He could tell this gentle man had the heart to fully love another man's child and give that child the family she deserved.

They fell into silence on the way up the hill to Gretchen's. Finally, Joe began speaking in a soft, melancholy voice. "I tried everything I could do to make Gretchen happy and want for nothing. When she picked Tony for a husband, I knew it was a mistake. The ladies in the family were jumping up and down. You should have seen Kate. She was a teenager with braces, popping her bands all the time eating candy. She idolized Tony."

"Hmm. She was about Clover's age then."

"Exactly! Right about thirteen, fourteen. Anyway the women at the church were going bananas over Tony and his NBA buddies, looking like a bunch of giraffes. I never liked the fact that he didn't seem to pay attention to what Gretchen was saying. Everything was a joke to him. But he was the fair-haired kid, the 'big catch' everyone wanted. They married, moved to Phoenix, and then up to Portland where his career really took off."

"I know what you're saying. But she was happy, so,

what are you going to do?"

"That's right. And just before Angie was born, he started being a little sloppy with his habits. Between you and me, I think he'd always been a player. But he had been good at hiding it."

Trace fisted his hand at the thought of Gretchen's husband treating her with such disrespect.

"You probably didn't want to interfere, I'm guessing."

"Got that right. Her mother would hear nothing about it. Insisted they'd work it out, and, well, as they say, the rest is history. She showed up one weekend with little baby Angie cuddled in a blanket and the other two girls with their teddy bears and suitcases. She had a black eye that her makeup didn't cover. We'd already seen the TV tabloid videos. She came home and spent about a month with us during that summer, and they were able to work out an amicable divorce."

"I heard."

"You know she hasn't taken a dime of his money?"

"She told me."

"What does that say about a person?"

"It means that she values her family and her relationships more than anything else in the world. You gave her that, sir."

"Well, I wish I could take the credit. But Gretchen landed on her feet and did just fine with those girls.

Not that it wasn't a struggle. After all those years, now she has to deal with this."

"I hope the attorney is a good one."

"Me, too."

They pulled up into the driveway. The girls ran around the side of their grandfather's car to give Trace a hug, each competing for the chance to give him a kiss. He got down on his knees and hugged them all.

"What am I, chopped liver?" Joe Morgan shouted.

"No, sir, you're the man that made all this possible," Trace said with a smile. He walked into the house, Clover carrying his bag while the other two girls held his hands, one on each side.

Gretchen was in the kitchen. When she turned around, the sight of her glowing face took his breath away. Her warm smile revealed a bit of shyness, and she raised her right shoulder, lowering her chin.

He cleared the space between them in three long steps. "Come on, Gretchen. You can't really be that shy, now." He hugged her and felt the luxury of her softness melting against his strength. He whispered in her ear, "After all the things we've done, you couldn't possibly be shy." He held her head in his palms, and she giggled. He slowly placed a proper kiss on her lips, and she wrapped her arms around him with complete abandon.

"Thanks for coming, Trace. I feel so much safer

now."

He was introduced to Louise Morgan, Gretchen's mom. The two looked like sisters.

"Forgive the dumb question, but weren't you supposed to be in court this morning?"

"No, it was just for the attorneys. I don't have to appear until later on, if things progress that far. We're hoping he'll just give up, if he sees we're fighting him."

Trace scratched his chin, not sure of the logic of her statement. He chanced a look to Joe, and he was not smiling. Joe knew. Ask a desperate man to be reasonable or give up, and what does he do? He gets worse. Trace had seen it over and over again.

Gretchen's phone rang.

"Hello?"

"Delmar Bernstein here."

"Wait a minute. I want to put you on speaker phone. The family is all around. Is that okay?" She did so without getting his agreement.

The speaker distorted his chuckle. "I guess so, if you don't mind. Everything's PG at the moment."

"So what's the news?"

"Well, we got a restraining order for sixty days. But they're demanding you submit to questions and an interview by the court. I agreed, with your permission."

The gathering in the kitchen cheered, especially the girls.

Delmar continued. "I wouldn't celebrate yet. I've got a list of things they're demanding to see. You're going to have to submit bank statements and the girls' shot records and physicals. They want an accounting of what you've spent over the years raising them. It's all intended to be intimidating. We'll help you prepare all this."

"Okay. But this is good news, right?"

Bernstein paused. "Gretchen, the opposing counsel told me she would be surprised if we were able to agree to terms in less than twelve months. Think you can hold out that long?"

She looked at her family, landing on Trace's face last. "I can do anything, if it means we'll win. I'm in it for the long haul."

"That's my girl. I have to read the judge's orders when it comes back to me tomorrow or the next day. We'll get together and strategize the next step. Now you keep your cool, and don't intimidate him. But if he does come by, you call the police and give them my number, day or night, understood?"

"Absolutely. Thank you Mr. Bernstein."

"You're very welcome, my dear. Bye, family."

The crowd echoed "Good-bye, Mr. Bernstein" back to him.

Gretchen hung up and threw herself into Trace's arms. He was delighted for her, and it made him feel wonderful seeing her so happy. But he knew that they'd just beaten the bees nest down out of the tree, and the coming horde would be arriving soon. He hugged her tight.

"That's wonderful, sweetheart." He and Joe shared a look over Gretchen's shoulder. He was glad he had a good, wise-thinking man as his second. He might need it.

CHAPTER 27

JOE AND LOUISE offered to take the girls grocery shopping, but Gretchen volunteered to go with Trace.

"I just need to get some air. I've been holding everything inside. Worried about everything for days now. I haven't been able to sleep. I just want to get out and breathe something outside."

"So we'll go shopping, and then you're going to lie down and take a nap," Trace commanded.

Gretchen gave him a flirty smile.

"No, I'm hands off. You need to take a nap and catch up. Time for partying later, my dear." He gave her a warm hug. It felt so good to have him back in her home, with her family. The world seemed a much more friendly place with Trace at her side.

He drove Gretchen's car to the organic food store. He pushed the cart. He picked up things she pointed to. She was having fun ordering him around like her personal servant, and he was playing along with it, a wry smile on his face. Everywhere they walked, women turned to get a better look at his enormous shoulders and slim waist. He seemed to be completely oblivious to it.

After the checkout, he offered to buy her an espresso at the coffee house next door. They stored the groceries in the car and then walked hand-in-hand to the coffee shop.

While Trace paid for the drinks, she waited at a table by the front window. She'd picked up the front page of the Oregonian and saw something about an upcoming trade for Tony. The article on the inside went into detail on his job performance, his problems at home, and an accusation from his fiancée of some roughness. This was good news. Gretchen folded the paper up and slipped it in her pocket. She studied Trace's handsome physique as he paid for the coffees and didn't notice the shadow covering the front doorway.

Tony grabbed her arms, yanking her to her feet so fast she was stunned and tried to scream, but his other hand clasped over her mouth. Gretchen tried to kick his ankles, his knees, scratch his arms, and pull back his fingers, but he was taller and stronger than she was, and he overpowered her.

"You think you can just send me packing? What,

you trading me in on a new model?"

He dragged her toward the parking lot.

She tried to get someone's attention, and several noticed the altercation but turned their heads and pretended not to see. Her muffled screams and panicked look did nothing to draw anyone to her defense. They were close to Tony's pickup.

His hand slipped slightly. He adjusted his grip to lift her up and throw her into the cab when she let out a full-throated scream.

"Trace!"

Through the glass windows of the shop, she could see him drop the coffees and run straight for them. A car driving by nearly hit him, but he didn't slow down, and as he reached the two of them, he lunged straight for Tony's neck.

"Where are you balls, man? Only sissies pick on women," Trace screamed at him while he tried to pull Tony's arms up and around his back. The left arm made a loud cracking sound, followed by Tony's scream of pain. The right arm, his dominant arm, took a swing at Trace and came amazingly close to his face. Tony's left arm hung limply by his side, but he was backing up, anticipating Trace's attack.

"You fuckin' Boy Scout. You trying to inch your way into my life, take over my girls, and fuck my wife?"

"You're just the sperm donor, asshole. It takes guts

to be a father. You don't know the first thing about it."

"The girls are mine. Gretchen's mine. She always will be."

"You dumped her, man."

"I dumped that worthless piece of—"

Tony was caught off guard by the impact of Gretchen's rather large purse hitting the side of his head and sending him to the ground.

Trace grinned, which made her mad. "Whoa, there. Take it easy. Let's slow this down a bit," he said catching his breath.

"I don't want to." She began to kick Tony in the arm that was misshapen, the arm he fell down against. His eyes were wild with rage, but finally, the pain got to be too much, and he collapsed onto the asphalt, unconscious.

Trace pulled out his cell and called 9-1-1. Tucking it back into his rear pocket, he watched Gretchen rebutton her blouse that had completely gone undone and straighten her hair. She noticed he was laughing at her, hands on his hips.

"Trace, this isn't funny. I. Did. Not Have Fun."

He crossed his arms and began to laugh full out. "No, sweetheart. But I did."

AFTER THE POLICE came, Tony was taken away by paramedics. They were assured he'd be held at the hospital and arrested upon discharge. Several witnesses showed up to give their information, verifying the account Trace and Gretchen gave.

On the way back to the house, Gretchen called her attorney, who was concerned but thrilled that Tony had completely bungled his own case.

She sighed, leaned back against the seat, and closed her eyes. She saw the men wrestling with each other, heard the loud crack as Trace broke Tony's arm, and then felt the satisfying thud as her purse hit the side of Tony's face. Her lips made a smile, and then she couldn't hold it in any longer. She began to laugh, and then she began to cry.

"Come here, you."

She leaned against him.

"Some day, when you're eighty and some punk tries to steal your groceries, you'll remember that purse action and you'll knock his head off. Won't that kid be surprised?" He grinned as her insides melted. "You're lethal."

"I have my moments."

"Moments? You call those moments? I think you have a future in mud wrestling. You ever see how those women throw themselves?"

She pulled back and stared at the profile of his face. "I'm guessing those pictures would be in some of your valuable magazines you talk so much about."

Trace held his hands out, splaying his fingers. "All gone, Gretchen. I donated them to the prepubescent population of the Capris Arms Apartments."

"Well, we could stop by Powell's on our way home."

Trace pulled the car over to the curb. "Now why would I do that when I got the real thing?" He kissed her tenderly.

"Ideas."

"Oh, I don't need any help with ideas. Trust me. I've been thinking about nothing else ever since I left."

"I've been the same way, Trace."

"So where does that leave us?"

He waited for her to answer, which she appreciated. She reached for his hand and held it between hers.

"Well, let's see. We've survived one kidnapping and an ex-husband gone berserk." She watched his eyes water. He didn't try to stop them, but let her see the emotions brimming inside him. "The chemistry was there that first day we met at the airport. It's here now, stronger than ever. I always said I'd only take one more chance if the right guy came along. Are you that guy?"

He grabbed her, wrapping his arms around her waist and kissing the sides of her face. Into her hair, he whispered, "You better believe it, baby. There's one little wrinkle of a problem, though."

She untangled from his embrace, worried.

He shrugged and made a mock wince. "We have to live in beautiful San Diego. I'm a SEAL, and I'm staying in. I accept you and your three daughters, and I'll treat them as my own, if they'll let me. But you gotta accept me as a SEAL."

Her heart warmed. There were lots of good memories in Portland. But her time there was done, truly done. "I think I'm ready for a new adventure."

"Yes, ma'am. One last thing?" He met her eyes, slowly grinning. "Promise me you'll never hit me with that purse."

"I promise."

Thank you for reading SEAL My Love, Trace and Gretchen's story. If you want to read the book that launched Gretchen's character and learn about the love story between Kate and Tyler, when Kate was flying to Portland to visit her sister and fell in love at first glance, then you need to read

SEAL Of My Heart

It's Book 7 in the original SEAL Brotherhood Series.

But if you know you gotta read all the previous books by Sharon Hamilton, go check out:

The Ultimate SEAL Collection, Vol. 1 (first four novels in the series with two bonus novellas)

or

The Ultimate SEAL Collection, Vol 2 (Books 5-7 in the SEAL Brotherhood Series.

ABOUT THE AUTHOR

NYT and USA Today best-selling author Sharon Hamilton's award-winning Navy SEAL Brotherhood series have been a fan favorite from the day the first one was released. They've earned her the coveted Amazon author ranking of #1 in Romantic Suspense, Military Romance and Contemporary Romance categories, as well as in Gothic Romance for her Vampires of Tuscany and Guardian Angels. Her characters follow a sometimes rocky road to redemption through passion and true love.

Her Golden Vampires of Tuscany are not like any vamps you've read about before, since they don't go to ground and can walk around in the full light of the sun.

Her Guardian Angels struggle with the human charges they are sent to save, often escaping their vanilla world of Heaven for the brief human one. You won't find any of these beings in any Sunday school class.

She lives in Sonoma County, California with her husband and two Dobermans. A lifelong organic gardener, when she's not writing, she's getting *verra verra* dirty in the mud or wandering Farmers Markets looking for new Heirloom varieties of vegetables and flowers.

She loves hearing from her fans:
Sharonhamilton2001@gmail.com

Her website is:
sharonhamiltonauthor.com

Find out more about Sharon, her upcoming releases, appearances and news from her newsletter:
sharonhamiltonauthor.com/contact/#mailing list

Facebook:
facebook.com/SharonHamiltonAuthor

Twitter:
twitter.com/sharonlhamilton

Pinterest:
pinterest.com/AuthorSharonH

Google Plus:
plus.google.com/u/1/+SharonHamiltonAuthor/posts

BookBub:
bookbub.com/authors/sharon-hamilton

Youtube:
youtube.com/channel/UCDInkxXFpXp_4Vnq08ZxMBQ

Soundcloud:
soundcloud.com/sharon-hamilton-1

Sharon Hamilton's Rockin' Romance Readers:
facebook.com/groups/sealteamromance

Sharon Hamilton's Goodreads Group:
goodreads.com/group/show/199125-sharon-hamilton-readers-group

Visit Sharon's Online Store:
sharon-hamilton-author.myshopify.com

Join Sharon's Review Teams:

eBook Reviews:
reviewcrewsh@gmail.com

Audio Reviews:
reviewcrewaudio@gmail.com

***Life** is one fool thing after another.*

***Love** is two fool things after each other.*

SERIES OVERVIEW

SEAL BROTHERHOOD SERIES OVERVIEW

SEAL Encounter (Prequel Novella)
Accidental SEAL (Book #1)
SEAL Endeavor (Novella)
Fallen SEAL Legacy (Book #2)
SEAL Under Covers (Book #3)
SEAL The Deal (Book #4)
Cruisin' For A SEAL (Book #5)
SEAL My Destiny (Book #6)
SEAL Of My Heart (Book #7)
SEAL My Love (Book #9)

BAD BOYS OF SEAL TEAM 3 SERIES OVERVIEW

SEAL's Promise (Book #1)
SEAL My Home (Book #2)
SEAL's Code (Book #3)
Big Bad Boys Bundle (Books 1-3)

BAND OF BACHELORS SERIES OVERVIEW

Lucas (Book #1)
Alex (Book #2)
Jake (Book #3)
Jake 2 (Book #4)
Band of Bachelors Bundle (Books 1-4)

TRUE BLUE SEALS SERIES OVERVIEW

True Navy Blue (prequel to Zak)
Zak (Includes novella above)

NASHVILLE SEALS SERIES OVERVIEW

Nashville SEAL (Book #1)
Nashville SEAL: Jameson (Books 1 2 combined)

FREDO SERIES OVERVIEW

Fredo's Secret (Book #1)
Fredo's Dream (Books 1 2 combined)

PARADISE SERIES OVERVIEW

Paradise: In Search of Love (Book #1)

SLEEPER SEALS SERIES OVERVIEW

Bachelor SEAL (Book #1)

BONE FROG BROTHERHOOD SERIES OVERVIEW

New Years SEAL Dream

GOLDEN VAMPIRES OF TUSCANY SERIES OVERVIEW

Honeymoon Bite (Book #1)
Mortal Bite (Book #2)

THE GUARDIANS SERIES OVERVIEW

Heavenly Lover (Book #1)
Underworld Lover (Book #2)
Underworld Queen (Book #3)

FALL FROM GRACE SERIES OVERVIEW

Gideon: Heavenly Fall (Book #1)

Box Sets

SEAL Brotherhood Series Prequel Novella, SEAL Encounter, and Book 1, Accidental SEAL, are available in a convenient digital box set format

SEAL Brotherhood Box Set 1

SEAL Brotherhood Series Prequel Novella, SEAL Endeavor, and Book 2, Fallen SEAL Legacy, are available in a convenient digital box set format

SEAL Brotherhood Box Set 2

SEAL Brotherhood Series Books 1-4 (plus 2 prequel novellas) are available in a convenient digital box set format

Ultimate SEAL Collection 1

SEAL Brotherhood Series Books 5-7 are available in a convenient digital box set format

Ultimate SEAL Collection 2

Golden Vampires of Tuscany Series Books 1-2 and *The Guardians Series* Books 1-3 are available in a convenient digital box set format

Immortal Valentines Box Set

Audiobooks

All of Sharon Hamilton's books are available as audiobooks narrated by J.D. Hart.

REVIEWS

PRAISE FOR THE SEAL BROTHERHOOD SERIES

"Fans of Navy SEAL romance, I found a new author to feed your addiction. Finely written and loaded delicious with moments, Sharon Hamilton's storytelling satisfies like a thick bar of chocolate." —Marliss Melton, bestselling author of the *Team Twelve* Navy SEALs series

"Sharon Hamilton does an EXCELLENT job of fitting all the characters into a brotherhood of SEALS that may not be real but sure makes you feel that you have entered the circle and security of their world. The stories intertwine with each book before…and each book after and THAT is what makes Sharon Hamilton's SEAL Brotherhood Series so very interesting. You won't want to put down ANY of her books and they will keep you reading into the night when you should be sleeping. Start with this book…and you will not want to stop until you've read the whole series and then…you will be waiting for Sharon to write the next one." (5 Star Review)

"Kyle and Christy explode all over the pages in this first book, *[Accidental SEAL]*, in a whole new series of SEALs. If the twist and turns don't get your heart jumping, then maybe the suspense will. This is a must read for those that are looking for love and adventure with a little sloppy love thrown in for good measure." (5 Star Review)

PRAISE FOR THE BAD BOYS OF SEAL TEAM 3 SERIES

"I love reading this series! Once you start these books, you can hardly put them down. The mix of romance and suspense keeps you turning the pages one right after another! Can't wait until the next book!" (5 Star Review)

"I love all of Sharon's Seal books, but *[SEAL's Code]* may just be her best to date. Danny and Luci's journey is filled with a wonderful insight into the Native American life. It is a love story that will fill you with warmth and contentment. You will enjoy Danny's journey to become a SEAL and his reasons for it. Good job Sharon!" (5 Star Review)

PRAISE FOR THE BAND OF BACHELORS SERIES

"*[Lucas]* was the first book in the Band of Bachelors series and it was a phenomenal start. I loved how we got to see the other SEALs we all love and we got a look at Lucas and Marcy. They had an instant attraction, and their love was very intense. This book had it all, suspense, steamy romance, humor, everything you want in a riveting, outstanding read. I can't wait to read the next book in this series." (5 Star Review)

PRAISE FOR THE TRUE BLUE SEALS SERIES

"Keep the tissues box nearby as you read *True Blue SEALs: Zak* by Sharon Hamilton. I imagine more than I wish to that the circumstances surrounding Zak and Amy are all too real for returning military personnel and their families. Ms. Hamilton has put us right in the middle of struggles and successes that these two high school sweethearts endure. I have read several of Sharon Hamilton's military romances but will say this is the most emotionally intense of the ones that I have read. This is a well-written, realistic story with authentic characters that will have you rooting for them and proud of those who serve to keep us safe. This is an author who writes amazing stories that you love and cry with the characters. Fans of Jessica Scott and Marliss Melton will want to add Sharon Hamilton to their list of realistic military romance writers." (5 Star Review)

"Dear FATHER IN HEAVEN,

If I may respectfully say so sometimes you are a strange God. Though you love all mankind,

It seems you have special predilections too.

You seem to love those men who can stand up alone who face impossible odds, Who challenge every bully and every tyrant ~

Those men who know the heat and loneliness of Calvary. Possibly you cherish men of this stamp because you recognize the mark of your only son in them.

Since this unique group of men known as the SEALs know Calvary and suffering, teach them now the mystery of the resurrection ~ that they are indestructible, that they will live forever because of their deep faith in you.

And when they do come to heaven, may I respectfully warn you, Dear Father, they also know how to celebrate. So please be ready for them when they insert under your pearly gates.

Bless them, their devoted Families and their Country on this glorious occasion.

We ask this through the merits of your Son, Christ Jesus the Lord, Amen."

By Reverend E.J. McMalhon S.J. LCDR, CHC, USN
Awards Ceremony SEAL Team One
1975 At NAB, Coronado

Made in United States
Orlando, FL
05 August 2022

20581803R00153